A CURSE *for* SAMHAIN

DAHLIA DONOVAN

HOT TREE PUBLISHING

A CURSE FOR SAMHAIN

THE SKELETON CREW PARANORMAL COZY SERIES

BOOK 1

DAHLIA DONOVAN

HOT TREE PUBLISHING

ALSO BY DAHLIA DONOVAN

THE SKELETON CREW PARANORMAL COZY SERIES

A CURSE FOR SAMHAIN | A FATAL AUTUMNAL STEW

THE GRASMERE COTTAGE MYSTERY TRILOGY

DEAD IN THE GARDEN | DEAD IN THE POND | DEAD IN THE SHOP

MOTTS COLD CASE MYSTERY SERIES

POISONED PRIMROSE | PIERCED PEONY | PICKLED PETUNIA | PURLOINED POINSETTIA

LONDON PODCAST MYSTERY SERIES

COSPLAY KILLER | GHOST LIGHT KILLER | CROWN COURT KILLER

HONEY BEAR COSY MYSTERIES

HONEY MEAD MURDER | HONEY BEE MURDER | HONEY MOON MURDER

STAND-ALONE ROMANCES

AFTER THE SCRUM | AT WAR WITH A BROKEN HEART | FORGED IN FLOOD | FOUND YOU | BY THE FIRE | ONE LAST HEIST | PURE DUMB LUCK | HERE COMES THE SON | ALL LATHERED UP | NOT EVEN A MOUSE | FARM TO FABRE | THE MISGUIDED CONFESSION | STUBBED TOES & DATING WOES

For information, contact the publisher, Tangled Tree Publishing.

WWW.HOTTREEPUBLISHING.COM

EDITING: Hot Tree Editing

COVER DESIGNER: BookSmith Design

MAP DESIGN: The Illustrated Page Book Design

E-BOOK ISBN: 978-1-922679-99-4

PAPERBACK ISBN: 978-1-923252-004

For my found family

SOUTH MYRDDIN

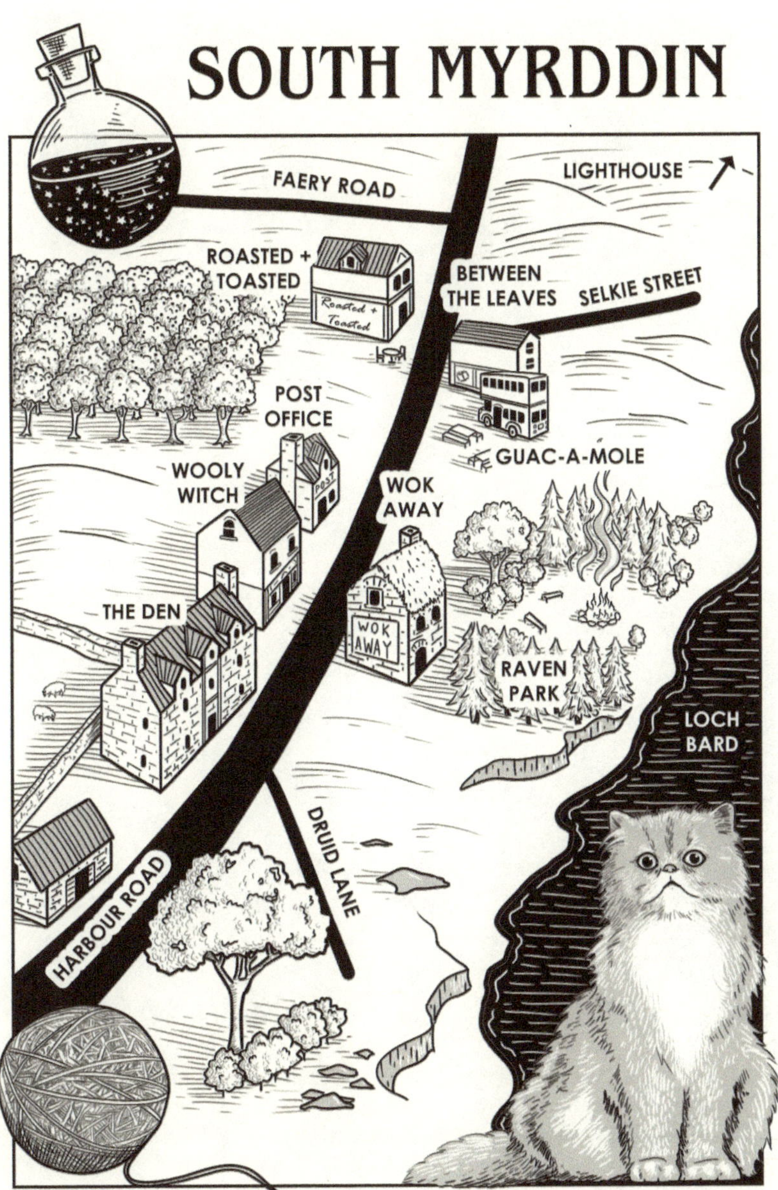

1

HYDE

"WHAT DO YOU THINK, MORTAR? PESTLE?" HYDE finished adjusting their button-down collar out of the blue sweater and glanced at the two cats observing them. One meowed quite loudly while the other sniffed before licking a paw. "You're both remarkably unhelpful."

The outfit of the day was one of their favourites. A lovely blue sweater with a well-worn button-down underneath. Jeans. A little boyish style from yesteryear with their trousers tucked into their socks and a vintage pair of brown boots.

I am a chubby ginger icon. I can seize the day.

Or I can seize a book to read.

That sounds better.

I'll seize a book.

A particularly loud yowl caught their attention. The cats were definitely ready for their breakfast. They both looked pitifully up at Hyde.

"All right. Come on, you two."

Mortar was a stunningly beautiful Persian with startling blue eyes who'd definitely been a queen in a previous life. Pestle, on the other hand, had probably been a court jester. His long ginger fur and almost glowing yellow eyes certainly set him apart, as did his sense of mischief.

They were Hyde's constant companions. They ruled the roost. And more often than not, they kept the right people in the shop and the rest from over-staying their welcome.

Between the Leaves had been Hyde's passion project for almost eighty years. The building had been a gift from the woman who'd taken them in as a child. A little shop with a comfortable flat on the second floor, it had once been a place serving after-noon tea, but books had been more interesting to Hyde.

Returning to stare at the mirror, Hyde attempted to corral their short, curly red hair into some semblance of a style. It was going to be a hat day. A *hat* day. It was a mostly nonverbal day. And a *they* day.

Being a vampire had its perks; being almost a

hundred yet having stopped ageing at thirty was certainly a plus. Being an autistic one, though, had drawbacks. Every sound and smell was amplified by what felt like a thousand. The world could be an incredibly overwhelming place. It was Flossie who'd come up with the idea for the signs.

Flossie Vandermark was one of the three witches who ran The Spiked Cauldron, the village pub. She also happened to be a proud member of the Skeleton Crew, a weekly knitting group who met up at Hyde's bookshop. Flossie had suggested a sign for days when Hyde didn't want to talk or when they felt more *they* than *she*.

It made Hyde feel accepted. Everyone wanted to do what made them comfortable. It was part of the magic of their village.

Acceptance.

Everyone knew about South Myrddin. The little village on a loch in the Scottish Highlands was founded by Merlin himself, or so the lore went. It had a reputation for taking in the abandoned.

Hyde had come as a child when their family vampire coven had rejected them. South Myrddin was the place for stragglers, odd ones, and outliers. A place to find family if one wanted.

A place to find home.

The village had a healthy coven of witches. A few

vampires. The odd werewolf. A collection of naiads, dryads, and brownies. Druids and shifters. A stray kelpie. An incubus and succubus, who were Italians who ran a restaurant. And one lone fae who'd been in South Myrddin since the beginning, or so they claimed.

The eclectic bunch of magical beings had all made South Myrddin their home. Most of the villagers came searching for a place to feel comfortable in their own skin. Hyde considered themselves grateful to have been left there all those years ago.

Making their way into the tiny kitchen in their one-bedroom flat, Hyde filled the cats' bowls before grabbing a bottle of blood out of the fridge. They ate regular food as well. A vampire required both to stay healthy, but sometimes they didn't have the energy for more than a drink in the morning.

After having a sip, Hyde sank into the plush armchair, enjoying the soft comfort of it. Everything in their flat had been geared towards not aggravating their senses. Nothing scratchy or pointy aside from their teeth. Nothing overly vibrant or colourful, just muted autumn tones surrounded them.

Their flat was more of an extension of the bookshop below or maybe vice versa. Copious numbers of shelves filled with antique tomes and the latest novels. Paintings and sketches of autumnal scenes adorned the walls. All of the armchairs were plush, mismatched and draped with the cosiest knitted blankets. There were little oddities and curiosities friends had brought from their travels.

It was perfect.

It was home.

South Myrddin could be quite insular by nature. While a reasonably self-sustaining village, the villagers maintained contact with larger towns nearby for things like the hospital, vet, and larger shops. Hyde never really saw the point of going anywhere else.

Hyde finished their morning beverage while idly watching Mortar and Pestle stalk around the living room. "Are you two coming? Or is there a shadow you want to hunt first?"

Mortar and Pestle followed them down the narrow carpeted stairs into the shop. Hyde immediately went over to pull back the heavy curtains, allowing the morning light to filter inside. Sun rays danced playfully through the stained-glass windows that had been a gift from their local glazier. The four panels across the front of the shop made up an autumn view of the loch and surrounding area. In the mornings, it made for a jewel-toned glow.

It was peaceful. Almost serene. And one of their

favourite parts of the shop. Hyde often lost themselves in the magic of it.

Faint burgundy lights twinkled all around the tops of the shelves. They'd been a present from Morrigan, one of the members of the local witch coven. She ran the village post office with her seeing-eye crow perched on her shoulder.

The lights never went out. Never dimmed. They twinkled merrily along the spines of the books like burnt orange leaves in the brisk October wind. It was all a part of the magic of home.

Grabbing a feather duster, Hyde did a quick whizz around the shelves. They didn't do a thorough cleaning—it made their skin crawl to touch certain cloths, and the smell of detergent burnt their throat.

Thankfully, the brownies who ran Feather Duster, the local cleaning company, were a dab hand at keeping the bookshop spotless. Isla, Lileas, and Fiona Lyall had all moved to South Myrddin years ago after a family illness struck the three of them. They didn't talk about it often, but the village rallied around them to help open their business.

Hyde flipped two signs on the counter, one from She to They and the other from Hello to Shh.

Stepping across the room to the record player stashed between two bookshelves in the back of the shop, Hyde put on one of their favourite Ambrose

Dance Band albums. The music immediately lifted their spirits. They picked Pestle up, playfully dancing across the floor to the sound of the '30s.

A sharp horn drew their attention outside. Teresa had obviously woken up. Hyde danced over to peer through one of the windows at the double-decker bus permanently parked to the left of the bookshop.

It was a lovely blue-and-cream vintage bus converted into a flat on the top floor and a taco truck on the lower. Teresa Vega had moved into the village from Ireland after her mother had passed away. Her father had gone back to Mexico practically the second after his wife had been buried but hadn't spoken with his daughter in years.

Teresa was the polar opposite of Hyde. Piercings, tattoos, long brown hair, and a devil-may-care attitude. She rode a vintage motorcycle and cooked the best mole tacos.

And Hyde had been hopelessly smitten from the first day they'd met the witch.

"Knock, knock." Teresa stepped into the shop still in her pyjamas, somehow managing to seem stunningly beautiful despite her rumpled state. "Fancy a coffee this morning?"

Hyde forced themselves to converse somewhat normally. It took effort to put a question together. "How's everything at Guac-A-Mole?"

"It's mole. Like mow-lay. Not like the annoying beast from *The Wind in the Willows*." Teresa groaned. "Mole like the sauce."

"I know. But I like saying mole."

"It's not Guac-A-Mole like whack-a-mole. This happens every time my Yank cousin visits, doesn't it?" She sighed dramatically, flopping down into one of the armchairs. By nature, she had a gracefulness Hyde never managed to achieve.

"The accent gets stuck in my head. Mole. Vole. Soul." Hyde couldn't stop listing words for a moment. They shook their head and tried to get their brain to not be their brain. "Sorry."

"Don't be. Oh, bollocks. It's a 'Shh' day. I didn't see the sign." Teresa leaned forward; her hand hovered over Hyde's arm but didn't touch them. "I'm so sorry. I'll tiptoe out and bring you tacos for lunch as an apology."

The cats followed Teresa to the door, then returned to Hyde, who hadn't moved. It was always refreshing to live in a village where everyone understood neurodivergence from personal experience.

Hyde wandered towards the front of the shop, staring out the window at the double-decker bus with a wistful sigh. They wished it were easier to spill their feelings.

Mortar rubbed against their leg.

"I'm aware I'm ridiculously obvious in my adoration. Someone will undoubtedly put a stake through me and spare me the heartache when Teresa turns me down. Okay, mildly dramatic. Maybe a splinter in my finger. Are you laughing at me?"

Mortar only purred in response.

2

TERESA

Teresa slumped back to the taco truck, feeling absolutely dreadful. She always tried to respect Hyde's quiet days, more than understanding with her own battles with anxiety. "I feel like such an absolute arsehole. How could I not look at the sign? It's literally on the counter. They're never going to want to talk to me again. Shite. How could I…?"

Rubbing her hands on her jeans, Teresa tried to reel her spiralling thoughts back in. She breathed through a sudden wave of nausea.

I'm being ridiculous. Hyde's my best friend. They're not going to be angry because I made an honest mistake.

With her heart racing and sweat on her brow, she made her way up the steps to the second floor of her bus. She immediately went to her work and ritual space at the front, just beyond the staircase. It had a

built-in desk with multiple cabinets below, along with an inset shelf above, leaving a wide swath of windows to allow light inside.

One half of the desk was for work, while the other was her ritual space. Practising her craft was one way she'd found to manage her anxiety. She grabbed a jagged piece of smoky quartz and a large brown candle, lighting it while murmuring the familiar Latin phrase to herself to release the nerves and bring in calm.

"Dimittis anxietatem et suscipe tranquillitas." Maybe it was the repetitiveness or the flickering flame of the candle or the way the light reflected on the quartz but with each repeat, she felt the slow release of anxiety and allowed calmness to take over.

Teresa ran her fingers across the flame, allowing it to dance between them. She'd always had an affinity for fire. The warmth also helped channel her anxiety. "It's going to be okay."

After a few moments, she felt the familiar calm settle over her. She snapped her fingers, and the flame vanished. Her nan had been the one to teach her how to ease her anxiety—and told her about South Myrddin.

Her nan. Her brilliant Irish grandmother who'd taught Teresa all about how to weave magic with word and song. A woman who'd shone brightly but longed for a place like South Myrddin to fly freely. She hadn't wanted her lone granddaughter to be caged in as she'd been by life, circumstances, and family obligations.

Nan Brigid had shown Teresa how to harness all the magic inside her. She'd taught her granddaughter to be herself, even when others didn't understand. It had also been why she'd sought out South Myrddin to begin with.

The home her nan had always wanted but never had.

All the family traditions and rich wealth of history had been passed down from Brigid. The cooking, however, had come from her abuela Lucia, who'd actually been her father's grandmother. A strong woman who'd taught Teresa the magic found in food. Both lessons had served her well over the years.

Returning to her altar, Teresa cleared everything away aside from one of the fresh beeswax candles she'd recently bought. It had been mixed with a few dried herbs and flowers—ones that had been special to both of the important crones in her life. She waved her hand across the wick, feeling the spark flame after a second.

I miss you both so much.

Teresa hovered in front of the candles for a few

minutes. She finally shook her head and stepped back from the altar.

Let's get going.

Deciding it was time to get on for the day, Teresa had a quick shower, then threw on a clean pair of jeans and a Wayward Hags long-sleeved T-shirt that she'd gotten at a concert. They were her favourite band.

Teresa scrambled down the curved stairs to the first floor of her converted bus. "Well, the tacos aren't going to make themselves."

There were no floating pots or flying utensils in her kitchen. Magic still found its way through every bite, though. Teresa often thought it might be handy if the tacos did make themselves, but alas, the family grimoire offered no insights no matter how often she read it.

She closely hoarded her family grimoire. The recipes held within the pages were well-guarded secrets, ones her abuela had passed down to her. It was her most prized possession.

Her only prized possession.

To get her family's mole recipe perfect took many hours and a ridiculous number of ingredients. Some had to be brought in especially by her supplier. The farm outside the village didn't have much need for multiple varieties of chillies. They did carry most of the other things she needed, though.

Teresa was elbow-deep into grilling chillies and making chicken stock when someone knocked on the bus door. "We're closed."

"Resa." Hyde's quiet voice was barely audible over everything happening in the kitchen.

"Just a second." Teresa wiped her hands on the towel draped over her shoulder. She flipped the chillies and then dashed over to open the door. "Come in, come in. Don't mind me. Must keep an eye on these so they don't get too charred."

"Can I help?"

"Can you break up all these discs of chocolate?" Teresa slid the Ibarra box over to them. "It'll save me time later."

"What's the difference between this and the bog standard we get here?"

"A little dark and a hint of spice from cinnamon. It adds a depth of flavour. Nothing else will do." Teresa began pulling the peppers off the griddle, transferring all of them into a pot of simmering water. "Makes for a lovely hot chocolate as well."

Hyde grabbed the first disc. They went to snap it and wound up sending little shards of chocolate flying around the kitchen. "What the dickens…?"

Teresa reached across with one hand and gently patted Hyde's arm. "Maybe a little less strength?"

"I'm so sorry."

"Don't." Teresa pressed her lips together, trying not to laugh. She made the mistake of glancing in Hyde's direction, and they both dissolved into giggles when a bit of chocolate fell out of the vampire's hair. "Don't apologise."

Hyde reached out and ran their fingers through their short red curls. They both snickered when another chunk of chocolate dropped. "I'm not sure I'm helping so much as hindering."

"It's not the worst disaster this kitchen has seen. Remember when I was doing the remodelling?" Teresa had done a lot of the work on her vintage double-decker bus herself with help. But she'd done all of the demolition herself. "I had paint and dust in my hair for what felt like months. I still find the odd speck where I didn't clean up from dumping it everywhere."

"Can't you wave your hand and make it all vanish?" Hyde smiled, then ducked their head down when Teresa glared playfully. "I know your particular brand of magic doesn't work that way."

"It'd be brilliant if it did."

"Yeah." Hyde shattered another chocolate disc.

Teresa watched them break one disc after another,

studiously avoiding everything but the chocolate. "Hyde? You okay? You don't have to force yourself to be social with me. Not that I mind the company. You're always welcome in my taco truck."

"Bus."

"You're always welcome in my taco bus." Teresa hesitated before reaching out. She didn't quite touch Hyde's arm but allowed her hand to hover. It let the vampire know she was there without trying to be pushy. "Always."

"Are you… are you coming to the knitting night?" Hyde gingerly broke apart yet another disc. "This evening? Flossie and Florence from The Spiked Cauldron promised to bring me some nibbles and a bottle of blood wine."

"I'd never miss an evening with you." Teresa gave them a teasing grin, but Hyde's attention remained on the growing pile of crumbled chocolate. "Or with the Skeleton Crew."

The Skeleton Crew had gotten its name from the scrimshaw knitting needles Hyde used for their projects. The set had been a gift from Florence Batch, one of the older members of the local witch coven. She'd been in the village for ages; Teresa had never dared to ask exactly how long.

Their knitting circle was made up mostly of the older members of the village witch coven. Hyde had been the one to start it. They'd all become quite close. The crones were very protective over their red-headed vampire.

"Do you ever think about your body?"

Teresa paused while dicing up some onion. She took a moment to process the change of subject. "No more than most, I'd imagine. What about you?"

Hyde stared intensely at the chocolate in their hand. "Yes and no. It's there. I often feel as though there's a moat between me and my body. Maybe that's why it takes me so long to process things or why I'm not particularly attached to the idea of gender. Just all rather confusing."

"Well, it's your body. No one else can dictate how you think or feel about it. Just do what makes you comfortable." Teresa had an autistic werewolf friend back in Ireland who'd once expressed a similar sentiment. She told Hyde a little about them. "You're not alone. Want me to put you in touch?"

"I'll think about it." Hyde gathered all the crumbled discs and dumped them into a spare bowl. "I'd better get back to the bookshop. Mortar and Pestle aren't exactly skilled enough to run the till if anyone pops in."

"They're a dab hand at keeping people in the store for longer." Teresa knew plenty in the village lingered at Between the Leaves for the cats as much as the books. "Anything new on the shelves? I saw several boxes being delivered yesterday."

"My book mystery. I didn't order any of them, so I've no idea what's inside." Hyde grabbed several spices off the shelves. They'd helped often enough to know what Teresa used—maybe not the quantities, but certainly the ingredients. "I figured I'd open them this evening. Flossie and Florence will want to check that no one's trying to harm me. You know how they are."

"Indeed. What exactly are they expecting to happen? The village is the safest place in the world." Teresa checked on the peppers in the pot. They needed a few more minutes before she could pull them out of the water. "Aren't you curious about the contents?"

"I am suspicious about the contents." Hyde wiped their hands carefully on one of the towels. "So, I'll see you later?"

Teresa knew they'd been inching closer to admitting their feelings for each other. She'd been patient, wanting to wait until Hyde felt comfortable enough to broach the subject. "I wouldn't miss it for anything. And no opening the box without me. I'm dying to know what's inside."

"Not literally."

"No, not literally. I promise."

3

HYDE

Hyde stepped out of the double-decker bus. They smiled at the door shutting behind them. The vintage vehicle made a particular sound that they enjoyed.

"Do you ever think about your body?" Oh my goddess. Why can't I ever be normal around her?

Shaking their head, Hyde decided to not think about having been stuck in the little kitchen on the bus with Teresa. It wouldn't do anything for their ability to function. Their feelings for the witchy chef definitely grew deeper with each passing day.

Nope. Not dealing with this right now.

Mortar was sitting on the rug by the front door when Hyde pushed it open. She immediately stood and flounced over to rub against their leg, leaving a trail of wispy silver hairs everywhere. A plaintive yowl was followed by the cat sauntering over to the

empty treat dish on the shop counter, only to be joined by Pestle soon after.

"You've had breakfast." Hyde caved under the pressure of their stare and fished out a packet of treats from one of the cabinets. "There. You've had your post-breakfast snack. That'll tide you over until dinner."

With the two furry menaces sated momentarily, Hyde turned their attention to their daily tasks. October tended to be a busy month, particularly towards the latter half. Between the Leaves carried a fair number of esoteric tomes; someone from within the village or nearby towns was always looking for something.

Combing through the shop messages, Hyde jotted down a list of books to find. They kept a detailed inventory, but sometimes, it was more enjoyable to search through the stacks. It made the day seem like a treasure hunt instead of work.

The day passed quietly. Hyde lost themselves in the older books in their collection. They only popped out when someone came in for a browse or a delivery.

"Anyone up for tea? I've got tacos."

Hyde set the book in their hand back on the shelf. They peered around the corner to find Teresa beset by cats. They paused to switch the sign from Shh to

Hello, for Teresa's sake. "You always have tacos. What time is it?"

"Lost track again, did you? It's late in the afternoon. You've got about an hour before the coven descends on you." Teresa held the container up and away from the scrambling cats. "These are my family version of Taquitos de Moronga. They're essentially blood pudding tacos. A little pickled onion, lime, chilli, and seasoned with my special blend. Think you'll love them. I've just been waiting for my supplier to come up with the perfect blood pudding."

Hyde blinked in surprise at the container pressed into their hands. "Thank you."

Teresa leaned in to brush a quick kiss against their cheek. "Anytime. Now, where's this box? I want to inspect it."

"Over there." Hyde pointed to the box and then opened the food. It smelled divine. Their senses were heightened both by the nature of their being a vampire and autistic. A double whammy. The food was a distraction from the sudden overwhelming shyness at the kiss. "No opening it."

"Fine, fine." Teresa waved off their concern.

Pestle followed Teresa over to the box in question. They carefully inspected it. Hyde took a bite of the first taco while watching the cat and witch stalk around the offending item. They poked and sniffed, doing everything but lifting it and shaking it.

"How's the taco?"

"Delicious is too mild a word." Hyde had inhaled the first one, barely having time to process how much they'd enjoyed it. "The best thing you've ever made me. Careful. He'll get ginger fur everywhere."

Pestle scowled back at Hyde as if personally offended by the accusation. Teresa plucked him off the floor and nestled her chin between his ears. They both returned to their observations of the box.

"I believe we've lost them to cardboard and mystery." Hyde offered a tiny sliver of the corn taco to Mortar, who'd deigned to move off the plush cushion by the window to join them. "I'm sure we'll figure out what's inside eventually."

"You could always open it. I'm not sensing anything foreboding about the contents." Teresa carried Pestle over, having apparently finished the inspection. "Aren't you the slightest bit curious?"

"Very."

"And?"

"The last time a mystery package arrived, it had a nasty surprise inside. And I'd prefer to avoid it." Hyde shuddered. As a vampire, they were relatively immune to most things. But the box had been triggered to catch fire once opened. It had only been the quick thinking of Santi Belrose, one of the local demons, that had saved them, the shop, and their beloved cats. "I'm not going to risk it this time. I want either Magali, Morrigan, or Santi to give it a thorough inspection before I open it."

"Did they ever find who sent the package to you?"

"It was ages ago, but I never heard anything. Trishna and Vidya handled the investigation. They promised to let me know if they ever found anything out." Hyde had a good relationship with most of the local police. The Jain twins had moved to the village from Bengaluru after issues with their family. They'd fit right in and eventually became local constables. "They were working with Santi. I'll ask him if he's heard anything."

Santi Belrose ran One Crafty Dimension, the local art and stationery supply shop. He was one of the few local demons. He hadn't fit in well with his family back home in Trinidad. His struggles with obsessive-compulsive disorder had made life difficult until he'd found a community that accepted him.

"He's handsome."

"Is he?" Hyde shrugged. They'd never really thought about it. "There's something of the windswept surfer about him. Not my type."

"Surfer?"

"Male." Hyde bit into their last taco, deftly avoiding an attempt from Mortar to steal a bite. "He's a decent friend."

"For a demon?"

"He's reformed." Hyde grinned irreverently at the long-standing joke that Santi always liked to throw out. "Plus, I think our surfing demon has his eye on someone else in the village."

"Do tell." Teresa immediately turned her full attention in their direction. Her deep brown eyes glistened with interest and mischief, making it suddenly hard for Hyde to think or breathe. "How have I missed the gossip?"

"People are too busy eating at your place. They linger here." Hyde focused on the taco and not the sudden swell of confusing emotions. The door swung open before gossip could be shared to reveal the man in question. "Santi."

"Hello, sweetie." Santi was, as always, immaculately dressed, not a hair out of place or a wrinkle to be seen. His light brown dreadlocks were pulled back out of his face, and startling green eyes stood out against his tanned skin. He always seemed as if he'd just stepped off a windswept beach. One could almost smell the salt in the air and hear the ocean waves crashing on the shore. "So, you got another box."

"Different handwriting." Hyde pointed to where Teresa had left it, sitting on one of the tables in the shop. "Different packaging, but yet another one I know I didn't order. There's no return address either."

"We'll figure it out." Santi patted their hand multiple times. He always did it an even number of times. "Anyone else been in yet?"

"Just us. Though, everyone's told me they'll be here." Hyde smiled when Santi tapped out another set of six before moving towards the package. Mortar and Pestle stayed away from him. They seemed to intuitively know their errant fur caused him stress. The demon often carried a lint roller in his pocket and was fastidious about using it. "I hoped you, Morrigan, and Magali might give it a once-over. "

"I'm sure Morrigan will help."

Teresa raised an eyebrow, glancing at Hyde, who smiled. She mouthed, "Morrigan," once Santi had turned his attention to the package. "Really?"

Hyde nudged Teresa's arm. "He can hear us."

"Yes, I can. No gossiping about me while I can hear you." Santi smirked when Teresa blushed. He ran his fingers across the box, covering every inch of it. "I'm fairly certain this one isn't going to spontaneously combust on you."

"Good to know." Hyde grabbed a pair of scissors

from behind the counter. "Safe to open, then? Or should I wait for Magali or Morrigan?"

"Safe to open." Santi rested his palm against the top of the package. "There's definitely something inside, but whatever it is, there's no malicious intent."

Hyde sneezed, shaking their head. "I can feel the air thicken when you do that."

"My apologies." Santi's smile made them think he was less sorry and more intrigued, as he always was at their reaction to his particular brand of magic. He finally grabbed his leather satchel and began pulling out his current knitting project. "I think I'll get a head start before the gossips get here."

"You enjoy it just as much as everyone else." Teresa had come over to sate her curiosity about the box. "Did you hear about what happened at The Spiked Cauldron yesterday?"

"No." Santi drew the word out while untangling yarn from his knitting needles. They were made from dark wood with script etched into it in a deep burgundy. No one had ever dared ask him about them. They had a slightly ominous feel to Hyde. "Did someone have too much ale and ask one of the crones out for tea?"

Hyde shook their head, moving over to the box and cutting the string tied around it. "The courage required to ask one of them out would be immense. They're terrifying. Lovely but intimidating."

"What's in the box? What's in it?" Teresa hovered off to their right, anxiously waiting for the package to be opened. She glanced behind her when Morrigan strode in with Odin perched on her shoulder. The crow guided her over. They all paused to greet the witch before returning their attention to the mysterious package. "What's in it?"

"Is she stuck on repeat?" Santi glanced up briefly from the shawl he'd started as his current project. He'd found his favourite of the armchairs in the knitting corner. It was an old leather one that he'd brought with him after his second time with the group. "Maybe you should open it before *she* spontaneously combusts."

Rolling their eyes, Hyde made quick work of removing the brown wrapping around the box. They cut through the tape and set the scissors to one side. Teresa was practically holding her breath in anticipation.

"If this is just a packet of promotional materials, you're going to be severely disappointed." Hyde grinned at the indignant huff from Teresa. "How are you more excited about this package than I am?"

"Because she's not expecting it to explode in her face," Santi interjected.

With a shrug, Hyde returned to the package. They opened the sides of the box and were hit by the scent of dust, leather, and old paper. The book or books had been wrapped in a midnight blue silk that was covered in a familiar silver crest.

A family sigil.

Their family sigil.

"Hyde?" Teresa had lost her almost bouncing energy and stepped closer in concern. "What's wrong?"

Santi set his project to one side and slid forward in his chair. "Sweetie?"

"This is my family sigil." Hyde traced the lines on the silk, almost afraid to open the delicate wrapping and discover what was inside. Their fingers trembled briefly while touching the knot that tied the fabric together. "I don't understand."

Teresa inched closer to them and brought a hand up to linger above their shoulder, offering a hint of comfort without intruding. "You don't have to see what's inside."

"Now it's *my* curiosity in need of being sated." Hyde had to know what the silk hid. And why was the scent of the box so familiar? "I know this smell."

Santi leaned in even further, narrowly avoiding toppling out of his chair. He inhaled deeply and pondered to himself for a moment. "Smells like your shop. Leather and book dust."

"Whereas he smells distinctly of sarcasm, soot, and a faint whiff of the sea." Morrigan broke into their conversation. She made her way over to sit comfortably in her preferred chair—a tufted velvet wingback that was a faded teal shade with slightly frayed edges. Her familiar and guide crow, Odin, was perched on her shoulder, always prepared to keep her pet human out of trouble. "What are we inspecting? Fill in the blind witch."

"I received another package." Hyde pushed it further down the table when Odin fluttered down to inspect it. They gestured to the swallow-like bird without feet. "There's a cloth with my family sigil on it. A martlet floating above a globe. A few other symbols inside the circle."

"And it smells—apparently," Teresa added helpfully.

"There's no evil intent aside from the man sitting over there." Morrigan jabbed her carved staff in Santi's direction, a bemused grin on her face. "I suspect you'll find answers within the cloth."

"Ah, yes, thanks ever so much for the insight," Santi snarked at her. The two loved to bicker back and forth.

Rolling their eyes at them, Hyde turned their

attention back to the mystery. They took a shaky breath and then reached out to carefully undo the knotted fabric. The silk was easy to unwrap, revealing a leather-bound book.

Hyde ran their fingers along the ribbed spine and the all-too-familiar sigil at the bottom. "You could say this is my family equivalent of a grimoire. There are no spells or potions. Maybe a few rituals, but mostly ones to pay respect to our ancestors. History. Stories. All manner of things. Each generation of Snodgrass vampire has added to its pages."

The Snodgrass journal had always been a distant memory for Hyde. They'd seen it once or twice when they were quite young before they'd been left to fend for themselves. The knowledge held within wasn't for them, according to some of their family.

"Hyde?" Teresa rested her hand on their shoulder, drawing them out of memories from the distant past. Ones best left forgotten if at all possible. "You don't have to keep or even open it. You don't owe them anything."

Nodding absently in response, Hyde placed their palm on the cover. The weight of history and power made their nose itch. They sneezed a few times, taking the handkerchief Morrigan tossed in their direction.

"Should we be seeing it?" Santi tapped out a

rhythm on his leg. He'd abandoned his knitting project on the table. "Family journals and grimoires are considered sacred."

"I was thrown out of the family. They didn't consider me at all." Hyde contemplated chucking the book into the fire. The only time in their career as a bookshop owner that they'd thought about destroying one. "Why should I consider anything related to them to be sacred?"

4

TERESA

Teresa opted out of the debate over opening the grimoire. She had a close connection with her own, and it didn't feel right to attempt to tell anyone what to do with theirs. Morrigan and Santi had gotten louder in the argument. They enjoyed sparring verbally, but it was easy to see Hyde growing increasingly uncomfortable. "Santi."

Nothing.

The demon and witch had clearly gotten lost in their conversation. A particularly sharp caw broke through the flirtatious arguing. Odin fluttered his wings before appearing to point towards Hyde. Santi muttered an apology before they both lowered the volume of their debate.

"Are we late?" Winifred Ferguson and Flossie Vandermark tried to shove their way into the shop at

the same time. The former finally stepped back and gestured magnanimously to the latter. "Age before beauty, darling."

With a withering glower at her business and coven partner, Flossie flounced into the bookshop. She paused to check the little signs on the counter before continuing to the knitting corner. The trio who ran the local pub were often confused for sisters, though they weren't related by blood. All three were somewhat frail, grey-haired witches with sharp senses of humour and surprisingly strong wills.

"Florence might be late. She didn't come to the pub this morning. She sent a note that she'd been ill last night." Winifred joined them. She set her over-sized satchel on the arm of her favourite chair, a plush pink monstrosity. It clashed horribly with the rest of the décor, but Hyde always refused to get rid of it. "She'd never miss the Skeleton Crew, though. I imagine we'll be treated to her dulcet tones soon enough."

"Are we knitting or nattering on about this book on the table?" Flossie chose her usual straight-backed chair. She set her quilted tote on the table. "And I'm not certain it's her stomach."

"Oh?" Hyde gingerly picked up the grimoire, returned it to the box, and set it on the bookshop counter. They'd obviously decided to deal with the mystery without a shop full of people. "Is she going to be okay?"

"The old witch is too stubborn to be anything other than okay. Don't worry, poppet." Flossie sounded completely unbothered. She opened her tote and pulled out a delicate lace shawl, which was her latest crochet project. "If Florence is ill, she's lovesick."

"Is she?" Santi's eyes gleamed with interest. He enjoyed gossip as much as everyone else. "Do tell."

"Old Angus Peck's been sniffing around." Flossie sighed when only Winifred seemed to know the man's name. "Florence fled an arranged marriage when she was quite young. She was head over heels in love with Angus from the moment they met here in the village."

"Until she wasn't," Winifred added in a loud whisper. "He was the one who got away. I never did get a straight answer about the ending of their relationship. She talks about him every once in a while."

"Especially after a rather strong glass of brandy." Flossie winked at Teresa. "I know she's coming because she's the one who promised to bring a few nibbles for everyone to enjoy."

"Maybe she just didn't want you nagging her to death," Winifred piped up once again with an interesting hint of gossip. "You were going—"

"Winnie. Not now," Flossie cut her off, to Teresa's surprise. "Why don't we get to knitting? Florence will be here soon enough."

With the matter settled for the moment, everyone got comfortable with their projects. Teresa wound up sharing the sofa with Hyde, which wasn't a surprise. It was what usually happened unless the vampire wanted space.

Hyde kept shooting glances towards the older witches, clearly having picked up on some of the tension between the crones. They leaned in closer after several uncomfortably quiet moments. "There's something going on, right? Not me imagining things. We've worked silently before, but it didn't feel like this."

"Definitely not your imagination."

"Right." Hyde tapped their finger against one of their scrimshaw needles. "Right."

"Sweetie?" Santi glanced up from his project when Hyde stood up. "Something wrong?"

"This." Hyde gestured around the room with the knitting needle. "Everyone's gone all quiet, but not the good way. You two are usually bickering like the best of old friends. Now you're all frosty, like the loch in the middle of winter. What's happened?"

Winifred turned pointedly towards Flossie, who

cleared her throat loudly. "Someone's being difficult."

Hyde tilted their head, staring at the two crones while Teresa could practically see the wheels turning in their minds. "Difficult how?"

"Well…." Winifred trailed off when Flossie clacked her knitting needles together. "We'll sort everything, poppet. Don't worry. Florence and Flossie had a few hairs out of place."

"Right." Hyde's gaze flicked between the two women once again before turning to Teresa, who shrugged. "Right."

Mortar and Pestle wound their way through the room, leaping up onto the couch and arranging themselves around Hyde. They'd obviously sensed their vampire's discomfort. The two cats got comfortable and then turned almost in unison to scowl at the older women.

It took all of her self-control not to snicker when the furry beasts managed to cower two of the most powerful crones in the village. The women made sheepish apologies, though neither seemed certain why. Santi winked at Teresa, not bothering at all to hide his amusement.

The rest of the knitting circle went smoothly. Two of their stray members had sent their apologies with Morrigan. Magali had to do stock at her yarn shop,

The Woolly Witch, while Zuri had begged off as well.

Zuri and her twin sister, Nsia, were naiads from Tanzania. Their family had lived near Kalambo Falls. The two didn't often speak about how or why they'd found their way to South Myrddin, but they'd made themselves at home, running the local fishery.

Teresa was good friends with both women. They'd frequently bring her some of their best fish. She'd gotten a message from Zuri that they were going out early in the morning on their boat, so she'd miss the Skeleton Crew.

Hyde shifted closer, carefully avoiding crushing the cat stretched out between them. "It's weird, right? The silence? Not the nice kind. This has edges."

"It's definitely not our usual brand of quiet," Teresa agreed readily.

The tension between Flossie and Winifred stood out. Santi kept sneaking glances at them. Morrigan had been suspiciously quiet, muttering to the crow on her shoulder while ignoring everyone else. Odin periodically flapped a wing against her head, letting her adjust her needles where required.

Their craft evenings usually lasted for hours. The chats could be lively or serious, depending on the mood. Food and wine flowed. But no one wanted to hang around tonight. Morrigan and Santi left together, with Flossie and Winifred going not long after.

Teresa breathed out a sigh of relief. The stony silence had been getting to her. "What in the world happened at The Spiked Cauldron? I've never seen those two so quiet. They're usually sharing every bit of gossip they've heard over the week."

"I'm worried about Florence. She's never missed the evening." Hyde gathered up their current project, putting it out of reach of the cats lazing on the sofa. "Should we check on her?"

Teresa checked the time. It wasn't super late in the evening. "Why don't we bring one of the new cosy mysteries you told me about? *Poisoned Primrose,* maybe? You know she loves to read them. There are still some chocolate cinnamon muffins left over in the taco bus. We'll take her a little care package if she's not feeling well."

"So it doesn't seem like we're just being nosy?" Hyde went over to one of the bookshelves in the new book section, hunting for something before finally grabbing a novel. "Here we go. This is one from her reading list."

Wrapping up the muffins in one of the spare napkins, Teresa waited for Hyde to get the cats corralled upstairs for the evening. The sun had just set, leaving the village in purplish darkness. She stepped outside to enjoy the crisp October air and the soft shadow settling around them.

South Myrddin had a mixture of quaint old-world charm and modern convenience. Most of the buildings had been around for at least a hundred years, if not significantly longer. The old gas streetlamps remained, though they were powered by magic no one had been able to change.

The witch coven always claimed Myrddin himself had created them, wanting his magical foundlings to never be stuck in the dark. Teresa wasn't sure she believed it. Much of the history of the founding of the village came down orally from one generation to the next; nothing had been written down about that time.

Teresa loved hearing the oral history, but it would've been helpful if something had been committed to paper.

She glanced back over her shoulder when the door opened. Hyde had pulled on one of their thicker cardigans. They had a stack of books in hand. "Ready?"

"I adore this time of day." Hyde ducked their head, smiling shyly when Teresa tucked her arm through theirs as they headed out for a walk. "It feels like the air tickles along my skin. Just a hint of magic in the air, dancing over me. It's always stronger as the sun sets."

"Yeah?" Teresa had always found rituals worked better around sunset, just another oddity about South Myrddin. "One day, we should write a book about the village and all the things that make it unique."

"Maybe." Hyde tensed beside her. "Not sure we should."

"Is there something I should know about the village?" Teresa had lived in South Myrddin for a while, but Hyde had been here for far longer. "Why is there no written history?"

"There are protections over the land and anyone who claims it as home." Hyde shuffled through the books in their hand. They held one out to Emrys, the local chemist and a druid, who'd lived in the village as long as anyone could remember. "I have your vampire romance."

"Ah. Bless you." Emrys grabbed the book, inspecting the cover. "I've been waiting for this one."

Emrys, no surname, seemed more like an aged fisherman with his short grey beard and wavy, shoulder-length hair than a wizened old druid. He'd always been quite fond of Hyde and protective of them. He frequently brought books back from his travels for the bookshop.

"It's full of so many stereotypes." Hyde sighed

dramatically. They grinned when Emrys held the book to his chest. "I've already preordered the next one in the series for you."

"You are always my favourite." Emrys reached out to pat Hyde's hand lightly. "You know—"

"Emrys, I don't want to hear about your relationship with some random vampire," Hyde cut him off before he could even start. Teresa opened her mouth to object but stopped when they held up their hand. "She might. But I've heard the story before—more than I ever cared to hear. The details were unnecessary."

"Someone had to give you the talk."

Teresa choked on a laugh, coughing a few times while Hyde pounded lightly on her back. "Emrys gave you the talk?"

"He volunteered himself, apparently." Hyde gave a full-body shudder. "It was educational."

"I have so many questions." Teresa glanced between the two, feeling equal parts amused, horrified, and curious. "But do I want the answers?"

"No, no, you do not," Hyde spoke over Emrys when he went to answer. "We made a pact. I get you all the romance novels, and we never ever speak about it again."

"Always so dramatic." Emrys gave their hand another pat. "Where are you two off to this fine evening? Aside from dropping off my latest novel?"

"Florence missed the Skeleton Crew this evening," Teresa answered when Hyde suddenly seemed lost in thought.

"Did she?" Emrys frowned. The smile slid off his face as he looked between the two of them. "Hurry along. Yes, definitely, hurry along to check on dear Florence."

Teresa had a sudden uneasy feeling building in her gut as Emrys spun around and stalked away. "That's… ominous."

"Incredibly ominous." Hyde nodded. "I think we should hurry."

5

HYDE

They strolled arm in arm down Harbour Road. It would've been romantic if not for the growing sense of worry. Hyde wanted to pick up the pace but couldn't think of a logical reason why.

Something about Emrys's reaction had jolted the both of them. They'd been silent since parting ways with the druid. He'd clearly sensed something.

"We're probably overreacting." Teresa broke the quiet as they crossed the road and started down Druid Lane, where Florence lived in one of the sweet thatched cottages. "Right?"

Hyde could only shrug. "I don't know. I just... I don't know."

They both came to a stop outside Florence's cottage. There were no lights on inside, which stood out. It was the only one along the lane in the dark.

"Hyde." Teresa pointed towards the front door. "Is it my imagination, or is it open?"

Hyde had better vision at night than Teresa and could easily see the gap between the door and frame. "It is. Ever so slightly. But it is."

"I don't like this." Teresa pulled her phone out of her pocket. "I'm giving Trishna a call. She's on duty this evening."

Nodding absently in response, Hyde left Teresa to call the local constable. They were drawn to the cottage. The open door. Florence's absence. The tension between her pub and coven partners. Something wasn't right.

Something just wasn't right.

Hyde walked cautiously up the short path to the door. The hanging lantern sent flickers of light bouncing around; it glistened off droplets on the ground. Crouching down, they realised it was clear. Someone had been watering the plants recently. "Florence? Are you there?"

"Hyde?"

"She's watered her plants recently." Hyde stood back up. They knocked on the door a few times and then rang the bell. "Florence?"

There was no response. Hyde pulled the sleeve of their cardigan down, not wanting to leave fingerprints when they pushed the door open. The cottage was dark. They listened for a moment, not hearing anything, before taking a few steps inside.

"Trishna said we should wait," Teresa said from the doorway. She still had her phone to her ear. "I'm calling Hamish. I know he's not working today, but he's an EMT. Surely, he could help."

Before Hyde could respond, a figure across the room caught her attention. They quickly found the switch on the wall and flipped on the lights. It took a moment for their vision to clear from the sudden brightness.

"Oh, holy fucking goddess," Teresa gasped. She dropped her phone, oblivious to it clattering to the floor at her feet. "Hyde."

"I see her." Hyde couldn't look away from Florence, who was slumped to the floor. She appeared to have been preparing to leave the cottage from the way she was dressed. A basket was beside her with scones and biscuits strewn across the floor. "Should we see if she's breathing?"

"Hyde? I'm not sure we should be in here." Teresa bent down to retrieve her phone. "I'm calling Trishna back. I'm guessing she'll want to get one of the investigators down here."

"I can't leave her alone." Hyde stared at the blank

face of the grey-haired witch who'd been so kind to them. There were scratches along her neck as though she'd been clawing at her throat. Her lips were blue but appeared swollen. "Her skin's icy."

"Hyde? Trishna said we should step outside. There's nothing we can do for Florence." Teresa spoke softly. She placed a hand lightly on Hyde's back. "There's nothing we can do for her."

"You said that twice."

"It bears repeating." Teresa stepped back, giving Hyde room to get to their feet. She slipped an arm around their shoulder. "Maybe she had a heart attack. I'm sure she…."

"She was poisoned." Hyde had no doubt in their mind. Florence had lived long enough to know if she had any allergies. Someone had done this to her. "This wasn't an accident or a heart attack. She was murdered."

"Hyde."

"I could smell something rotten." Hyde buried their grief and the ache in their heart underneath a myriad of swirling thoughts. "Acrid. Bitter. And it wasn't death. Not just that, though. There was a floral and sweet note as well. The combination made my stomach churn."

"You're sure?" Teresa held a hand up when Hyde glared.

"The scent of death and decay doesn't change. This was different. Never smelled anything like it." Hyde allowed Teresa to lead them out of the cottage. They stood on the path, both unsure of what to do. "Who'd want to murder Florence?"

"It could've been an accident."

"It wasn't." Hyde had never been so certain of something in their life. They couldn't help repeating themselves. It was starting to become overwhelming. "She didn't have a heart attack or a stroke. This wasn't an allergic reaction. Someone did this."

There were so many questions in Hyde's mind. Had Emrys sensed something was wrong? Who would want to kill Florence?

"You don't think Flossie or Winifred would…." Hyde couldn't bring themselves to finish the sentence. "They wouldn't."

"Let's not jump to any massive conclusions," Teresa cautioned, but Hyde had a feeling she didn't necessarily believe that herself. She'd finally put her phone away after sending a message. "Oh. There's Fynn."

Detective Inspector Fynn Baines had arrived before the constables. His long dreadlocks were pulled back from his face, showing off the tattoo on his neck and the seer mark on his left temple. "Jekyll. Ms Vega."

Hyde usually smiled at the nickname. Fynn was one of the few people who called them Jekyll. "You couldn't see this?"

"Cariad," Fynn spoke gently. He'd inherited his Welsh father's easy-going nature and his Ghanaian mother's ability to see aspects of the world, both future and past, with varying measures of clarity. "You know it doesn't work on demand."

"They killed her," Hyde hissed. Anger and sadness warred inside them. "They killed her, Fynn."

"I promise to do everything in my power to find out what happened." Fynn had a calm energy about him. He was one of the few people in the village whom Hyde always felt relaxed around. "But first, I have to investigate."

"How'd you get here so fast?"

"I was having a late meal at Wok Away." Fynn lived in a much larger village about twenty minutes away from South Myrddin, as did most of the police who covered their little home. "They have the absolute best crispy duck pancakes and roast pork. I was feeling extra carnivorous this evening."

Wok Away was one of the few restaurants in their little village. Evelyn and Lee Tham were fox shifters from Beijing who'd found their way to South Myrddin ten years earlier. They'd been a much-welcome addition.

"The twins and Nastia should be arriving shortly." Fynn broke into Hyde's thoughts, drawing them back to the conversation. "If your instincts are right, I'll probably be calling in the chief inspector as well. I've got the coroner on the way. Why don't you two have a seat in my vehicle? Get yourselves warm. It's going to be a long night, and I've a few questions I'll want to ask once I've assessed the scene."

Nothing made sense. Hyde ignored the invitation to sit in Fynn's vehicle. They wandered over to sit on a bench underneath the fruit tree in Florence's front garden. There were delicate lights dancing along the branches.

Staring up at the lights, Hyde thought about Florence, Flossie, and Winifred. They could be sharp and acerbic, all three of them. But they'd also helped a young vampire find their way in a new place.

Their chest hurt. Hyde rubbed their palm over their heart, trying to ease the pain. Spots appeared in front of their eyes with each short, panicked breath.

"Hey, hey." Fynn knelt in front of them after a few minutes. He snapped his fingers in front of their eyes repeatedly while lightly patting their hand. "Take a breath. It's going to be okay. Did you touch anything in the cottage?"

"I…."

"Did you touch anything that might be poisoned?

Are you suffering from an anxiety attack? Or is it possible you've come in contact with something tainted from the cottage?" Fynn rubbed their hand. He frowned in concern when Hyde couldn't answer. "All right. Odds are you aren't likely to be harmed by what would hurt a witch. Can you tell me what you had for breakfast?"

"I… don't remember." Hyde attempted to slow the swirling thoughts. It was as though their head were spinning around like a top. They wanted nothing more than to reach up and make everything stop. "Probably tea at some point."

"Good, good. And how were your furry familiars? Did they have tea?"

"No," Hyde retorted indignantly. "Not sure they or I could handle those two overly caffeinated."

"True enough. I'm pleased to see your breathing is returning to normal." Fynn sat back on his heels, giving them some space. "Now, you're sure you haven't touched anything inside."

"Aside from the light and Florence to make sure she was…." Hyde couldn't complete the sentence. It seemed so terribly final to say "dead." "I didn't touch anything around her. I was right, wasn't I?"

"The inquiry has barely begun. But my instincts tell me you're correct." Fynn gave their hand a squeeze. He stood up and brushed his pants off.

"Prepare yourself. I've had to call the detective chief inspector since he has close ties to the coven leadership. He'll be here shortly. I've got other constables here now to cordon off the scene for me."

"Balls," Hyde cursed. "Why?"

"He's not that bad."

"He hates me." Hyde dragged their fingers roughly through their short red hair. "He'll probably think I did it."

"Hyde."

Hyde scowled at Fynn, who raised an eyebrow. "Can you honestly tell me he doesn't hate me?"

"He doesn't hate you." Fynn glanced over his shoulder towards one of the constables calling his name. "I have to get back inside. Try not to pick a fight with my boss—and the leader of the Highlands vampire coven."

"Not my boss. Not *my* leader." Hyde nodded when Fynn simply raised an eyebrow. "I'll do my best."

Jonatan Pacheco was an old vampire. Possibly one of the oldest in Scotland. Hyde had never conformed to the coven rules. They'd never attempted to join or participate. Truthfully, they wanted nothing to do with them.

It had reminded Hyde far too much of their family coven who'd abandoned them, which maybe hadn't been fair to the local one. Jonatan had seemed to take it personally. And he never missed an opportunity to remind them.

"Hyde." Fynn tapped a finger against their hand. "Just ignore him."

"I'll do my best," they repeated.

6

TERESA

FLORENCE BATCH HAD BEEN IN THE VILLAGE FOR A LONG time. She was one of the elders of the coven. So, it didn't surprise Teresa when Detective Chief Inspector Jonatan Pacheco arrived an hour or so after his detectives.

What surprised Teresa was his sneering immediately at Hyde, who raised their upper lip, revealing sharp teeth in a sign of aggression she'd never seen from her friend.

What the devil is that all about? There's some history I've clearly never heard.

Hyde tended to be polite to a fault or at least skilled at ignoring people. "Jonatan."

"Mx Snodgrass."

Teresa sidled up next to Hyde. She looped her arm through theirs and smiled charmingly at the elder vampire. "Detective Chief Inspector Pacheco. Lovely to see you."

"Hmm. Is it?" DCI Pacheco's gaze didn't leave Hyde, who in turn seemed to be glowering at the chain around his neck. "I understand you received a family heirloom today."

"And I understand it's none of your business." Hyde tensed beside her but didn't waver. "Who told you?"

"A concerned—"

"Busybody? I don't have to talk to you or anyone else about what arrived at my shop." Hyde nodded towards the cottage where two constables, two detectives, and the coroner were all watching. "Shouldn't you be doing whatever it is a chief does at a murder scene?"

DCI Pacheco glanced over and muttered a few choice curses in Spanish that had Teresa practically choking herself to keep from bursting out laughing. He sighed loudly. "One day, you'll realise all I want to do is help you as I help any vampire in Scotland."

"And maybe one day, though we've got seven decades to the contrary, you'll acknowledge I've never asked for your help." Hyde had gone from tense to anxiously vibrating with an undercurrent of emotion. They turned to point across the street to a bench in front of another cottage. "I am going to sit over there."

"Mx Snodgrass."

"I am going to sit over there." Hyde acted as though they hadn't heard him, walking across the lane and practically throwing themselves down. "This is me. Sitting down. Over here."

Teresa couldn't restrain her smirk when she glanced back from Hyde to meet DCI Pacheco's eyes. "It seems they'll be sitting over there."

"Ms Vega." DCI Pacheco finally stopped glowering in Hyde's direction. "I understand you hail from the same region of Mexico that my father did."

"My father does. He doesn't claim me."

"Ah." His silver eyes flickered over to Hyde once again. "A familiar story in South Myrddin."

"Yes. Maybe something you should consider before you irritate Hyde for the hundredth time." Teresa scratched her jaw absently before rubbing her thumb over her lip ring. "They deserve better from the community that's supposed to welcome them."

"I tried. Mx Snodgrass is rather sensitive."

Teresa narrowed her eyes. "Hyde's autistic. So maybe you have to—"

"Hyde can hear you from the bench," Hyde cut her off mid-sentence. "And Hyde doesn't appreciate being talked about like they're not here. And Hyde doesn't enjoy speaking in the third person, so they're going to stop."

"Boss? You should see this." Detective Inspector Baines provided a much-needed interruption. "We may have found something."

Taking advantage of the distraction, Teresa darted across the lane to sit beside Hyde. They watched the police confer by the front door of the cottage. Hyde leaned forward, obviously attempting to listen.

Hyde shifted closer to Teresa. They spoke in a barely audible whisper. "They found two cups in the sink. The teapot was sitting on the counter. Fynn thinks it's possible someone got poison into the tea somehow."

"What do you think?"

"I think I need to check some of the plant encyclopaedias and deadly plant books in the shop. The scent I picked up was unique. If it's some kind of flora, it has to be a rare species." Hyde stared off down the lane for several seconds, likely trying everything possible to not think about Florence being gone, pushing off the mourning and grief. "Maybe *Medicinal Herbs and Poisonous Plants*. I'm fairly confident I've got a first edition somewhere in the shop."

They fell into a morose silence again, watching the police work. After what felt like hours, Constable Trishna Jain jogged over to them. She got some basic details from them before telling them to go home. The detectives would apparently have more questions later.

"Do you really want to go home?" Teresa asked after they'd walked so slowly down the pavement that they were almost going backwards. "Why don't we head to The Spiked Cauldron? I know the coven will probably gather to pay their respects to Florence. I've no doubts news of her death has already spread."

Hyde lifted the book in their hand. "She never got to read her last book."

"You could always give it a read tonight."

"I… maybe not this one." Hyde clutched it to their chest. "But you're right. The pub is a good place to be tonight. Not sure I could close my eyes without seeing her face."

They weren't the only two to be walking through the village. Members of the community slowly joined their procession to The Spiked Cauldron. The lamps around the pub seemed to burn brighter as if they knew Florence was gone.

Music bubbled up within Teresa. She'd always found it to be the perfect medium of expression. The words to one of her family's funeral dirges sprang to her mind.

Starting out at almost a whisper, Teresa sang out

the sadness in her heart. By the time they stepped into the pub, her voice was practically a roar above the hushed crowd. The words were wrenched straight from her soul.

In the corner of the room, someone had picked up a fiddle to accompany her. A guitar joined in not long after. And finally, the sweet sounds of a pipe came as Teresa repeated the first verse.

Most of the time, when Teresa sang in the pub, it was fun and joyful. A distinct sorrow weighed on everyone tonight, though. She moved through all the songs that seemed to fit the mood.

After singing "Bonny Portmore," one of Florence's favourites, Teresa stepped out of the spotlight. She was exhausted. Physically and spiritually. Magic always flowed through her when she sang. It was why she tended to be the witch called forward when the coven lost someone.

When Teresa slid onto an empty spot at the bar, Hyde was beside her in an instant. They set a mug in front of her, nudging it closer until she picked the tea up. The scent of honey, lemon, and herbs hit almost instantly.

Teresa took a grateful sip of the soothing warmth, enjoying the easing of the rawness of her throat. "Thanks."

"Drink up. And then I'll take you home."

"I should…." Teresa nodded towards where the impromptu music group were still playing their hearts out.

"You've given enough." Hyde patted her on the shoulder lightly. "There's no point in exhausting yourself. Florence wouldn't want it."

From their spot at the end of the bar, Teresa had a good view of the gathered mourners. To her surprise, neither Winifred nor Flossie was here. One of the bartenders seemed to be running the pub in their absence.

"Hyde?" Teresa leaned in closer to avoid being overheard. She hoped the music and conversation prevented the supernatural ears of some from eaves-dropping. "You notice who's missing?"

"Flossie and Winifred." Hyde grabbed their glass of blood wine. "I thought maybe they didn't know, but Maud said they do. It's strange, right? Them not being here?"

"Everyone grieves in their own way." Teresa wasn't necessarily sure she believed her own words in this case, though. "Right?"

"Right."

7

HYDE

The crowd at The Spiked Cauldron continued to grow. Teresa had begged off singing another song, so Amalia Bassani had picked up where she'd left off. The succubus had a hauntingly beautiful voice that harmonised almost hypnotically with her incubus partner, Battista Sartor.

The incubus and succubus had been in the village for years. They ran an Italian restaurant, Al Dente. Hyde had been on the hunt for an ancient Roman manuscript for the two for a decade with no success so far.

While many in the crowd swayed to their lament, Hyde had to duck outside. The slightly high-pitched tone of Amalia's voice grated on their nerves. It was as though a thousand tiny thorns pricked at their ears.

Covering their ears with their hands, Hyde stumbled across the lane and dropped onto the bench in front of the post office. The sky had cleared up, offering a lovely view of the stars. It had turned cold.

Somehow, it seemed fitting for the moon to be high above and the air to be so crisp and biting. A howl echoed in the night; somewhere in the distance, another answered. The weres had obviously heard about Florence's death. Each member of the village mourned in their own way.

"Cariad? Everything all right?" Fynn crossed the lane to join them. He waited until they nodded to the empty space on the bench to take a seat. "The scene examination team are combing through the cottage. Chief Inspector asked me to keep an eye on the crowd here. Was it getting too much in there for you?"

"A little." Hyde paused when Fynn nudged them with his elbow. "Maybe a lot."

"Anything stand out to you?" Fynn reached into his pocket and eased out a knife along with a small piece of wood. He began to slowly whittle away at it. "Amongst the crowd?"

"I'm not a detective."

"Maybe. But you've a keen mind and are more observant than anyone I've ever met." Fynn lifted the wood up to the light from the lamp before returning to his carving. "So?"

"Winifred and Flossie are both absent. It's odd."

"Grief hits some differently."

"True, but every other time, they'd be either behind the bar or seated at their table." Hyde couldn't shake the feeling that something was off about them. "I was planning to head back to the shop. I don't want to leave Mortar and Pestle alone too long."

"Afraid they might take over the world?"

"Or order themselves a mountain of treats." Hyde managed a small smile. They didn't have it in them to give a full laugh. "Thanks, Fynn."

"Take care of yourself, Jekyll. Try not to get yourself into trouble." Fynn waved absently at them while focusing on his carving. "I'll talk to you tomorrow at some point, I'm sure. Anyone gives you a hard time, you send them my way."

Deciding not to question the slightly ominous tone of his warning, Hyde said their goodbyes and made their way back to the bookshop. They opened the door to the upstairs flat, allowing Mortar and Pestle to join if they wanted. Despite how tired they felt, the herbalism shelf beckoned.

Odds were if a book held the answer to the mystery of Florence's death, it was likely to be in the herbalism section. That area contained every tome on the uses of plants and plant extracts in their shop, including several on folk medicine.

But Hyde wasn't searching for a way to get rid of the flu or a random wart. They wanted to know what had killed their friend. Their instincts told them a poison of some sort—and it was more likely than not to be of the plant variety.

Perusing the shelves, Hyde pulled out any book that might be even remotely useful. They even grabbed a picture book meant for little witches and druids. It had colourful pictures and fanciful tales about each plant.

With the books spread out across a little table near the counter, Hyde grabbed their laptop. Technology had come more slowly to South Myrddin, but they'd embraced it fully. It certainly made doing inventory far simpler.

"Easy there, Mortar. No damaging the books." Hyde rescued the tome from the cat where she'd been pawing at the corner. They paused to read the title. *"So You Think You've Been Poisoned? A victim's guide to an untimely death.* Well, well, well, what a brilliant kitty you are."

Before Hyde could open the book, a tentative knock interrupted their praise of Mortar. Not to be outdone, Pestle traipsed over and opened the door for Teresa. The witch stared down at the cat and then looked up in surprise.

"Don't ask me how. They refuse to stay trapped unless they want to do so. It might come in handy one day." Hyde shrugged. "They never stray too far."

"I've brought some sort of pastry from The Golden Puff. The ones with the red droplet are for you." Teresa uncovered the platter, setting the linen cloth to one side. "Rosa insisted. An apology for her relative?"

"She's the niece of Detective Chief Inspector Pacheco." Hyde grabbed one of the round tartlets. It had a lovely sheen across the tops of sliced plum. "Ah, her bloody plum tarts. She makes these every Samhain for the vampire coven and always sneaks me a few. They're delicious. Not sure how she makes the blood caramel, but it's divine."

"I'll take your word for it." Teresa pushed the plate closer after grabbing what looked like a fried pastry roll of some sort. "These are casadielles. I think Rosa has her own family recipe. They're different from what I've had before in Oviedo. These have the usual walnut filling, but she's added cinnamon, ginger, and cloves."

The Golden Puff was the only bakery in South Myrddin. Rosa Pacheco had been in the village for longer than Hyde. She'd also ignored her uncle's strongly worded invitation to join the vampire coven; the two did not get along. But she seemed to enjoy the other members.

Finishing up the tartlet, Hyde decided to put on one of their records. The music would drown out the crackling sound from the lights above the bookshelves. It didn't always bother them, but when it did, they found it impossible to ignore.

After wiping off their fingers, Hyde flipped through the records. They grabbed one of the albums from Druids Song and put it on the player. The group did a mixture of instrumental folk and classical music, which fit their mood perfectly. The fiddle, harp, and flute melded well together.

Teresa finished up her pastry and set the plate off to the side. "So, what's all this?"

"Books."

"Is this Druids Song?" She closed her eyes and swayed to the music briefly before returning her attention to the books on the table.

"It is Druids Song. Their first album. Fynn gave it to me ages ago." Hyde set the record sleeve down and turned towards Teresa. "It's one of my favourites."

"What exactly are we looking for in these books?" Teresa shifted back in her seat when Pestle leapt up into her lap. She ran her fingers lightly over his head. "A poison local to Scotland?"

"Not a bad place to start, but also something with a bitter smell. Maybe even non-magical plants. A fast-acting one." Hyde returned to their seat only to find Mortar had claimed it for her own. They lifted her up and set her on their lap. It was a relief to not have to fight to be believed. "I'm never going to sleep tonight. This, at least, is something I can do."

They settled comfortably going through the books. Music and purring were the soundtracks of the evening. Hyde snuck glances at Teresa periodically, who occasionally lifted her head to smile. It was so comfortable and companionable, time seemed to slip away from them, and hours passed.

Hyde cuddled Mortar to their chest, their eyes filling with tears thinking about Florence. "I'm going to miss her."

"Me, too, though I didn't know her nearly as well as you did." Teresa reached out and gave Hyde's hand a squeeze. "Why don't I make some tea? We could use a break. All these plants are starting to blend into one another."

Hyde swiped the tears away with their cardigan sleeve. Mortar leapt to the floor and up onto the chair with Pestle. The two cats curled up together, a purring engine of contentment. "How did Florence miss the smell?"

"Not everyone has a nose as strong as yours. She might not have noticed anything unusual." Teresa went over to the little corner behind the counter where Hyde kept the kettle and basic supplies for tea and coffee. "In fact, I'd wager she didn't smell the poison. I didn't notice anything from where I stood."

Hyde pulled the beanie off their head and dragged their fingers through their short red curls, trying to detangle them. "Fynn might not have either, but there are at least two vampires and a shifter in the local police. One of them has to have picked up the scent I did."

"Maybe not Pacheco. Not sure he'd notice anything." Teresa shook her head. "I'm being unfair. He's an excellent police detective but a dreadful vampire." She grabbed two mugs, dropping teabags into them. "We'll go with simple. I know you've got the fancy blends, but these do in a pinch."

Hyde shrugged. They weren't feeling particular about what they drank. "There's the hot chocolate mix you got me behind the masala chai packet."

"Ah, brilliant. Perfect." Teresa put the teabags back and shifted things until she found the hot chocolate. "We don't have to solve this tonight,

Hyde. I'm sure the police would say we don't need to do it at all."

"It's Florence." Hyde knew Teresa was correct. Fynn might be the only person who wouldn't mind them poking around as long as they didn't disrupt the police inquiry. "I can't not do something."

"I know." Hyde joined Teresa by the little tea station. They put one of the mugs away and grabbed their favourite. It was autumn-themed with glorious jewelled tones. "Florence gave me this one. I had to glue the handle back on when Mortar knocked it off the table."

Stepping closer to them, Teresa looped her arm around Hyde's shoulders and gave them a squeeze. They watched the electric kettle for several minutes until it finally finished boiling. She poured the water over the hot chocolate mix she'd portioned into the mugs.

"I just feel like I have to do something." Hyde stirred their hot chocolate absently, leaning against the shop counter. "If I don't occupy my mind with plants and poison, I'll be consumed by the vision of her dead on the floor."

They took their mugs over to the knitting corner. Hyde found themselves drawn to Florence's favourite chair. They tucked their legs up underneath themselves and cautiously sipped the hot chocolate.

"Do you really think someone in the village is capable of murdering?"

"Just about anyone is *capable* with the right motivation. It's not capability that's the decider." Hyde knew they were being pedantic. "Willing is the word. I'm able to kill someone, but I'd never actually commit murder."

"I thought you were supposed to be the optimist."

"We live in a village meant for those abandoned or discarded. We've both seen the worst people have in them." Hyde shifted in the seat to allow room for Mortar and Pestle to join them. "It would be foolish to pretend the ability to commit a horrific crime doesn't exist in the average person. Monsters aren't the only ones to be afraid of in the world."

"Well, that's ominous." Teresa clutched her mug in her hands. "I mean, you're not wrong. But bloody hell, it's a terrible thing to consider."

8

TERESA

By three in the morning, Teresa struggled to keep her eyes open. Her head hovered inches above the book on the table. The words blurred together until she couldn't decipher a "the" from a "venomous."

"Hyde? I'm throwing in the towel."

"What towel?" Hyde lowered the practically ancient tome they'd been reading intently. They stared blankly at Teresa for several moments before nodding. "Ah, metaphorical towel. Sorry. What time is it?"

"Three." Teresa carefully shifted Mortar out of her lap onto a nearby pillow. "I'll need to be up in a few hours to food prep the truck."

"Bus."

"Technically." Teresa grinned. She walked around the table, placing a hand on Hyde's shoulder and dropping a kiss on top of their head. "Was that okay?"

Hyde tilted their head to the side, offering a shy grin before returning to the book. "It was."

"Why don't we have tea tomorrow night after you've closed up for the day?"

"To keep looking for poisons?"

Teresa was torn between amusement and frustration at how Hyde had missed the point. "Why don't we call it a date with a side of poison?"

"Fynn would say that's an indictable offence."

"A date with a side of researching potentially poisonous plants." Teresa maintained her serious façade for a second before they both dissolved into giggles. She clutched the top of the chair, using it to support herself. "I'm too tired for this. I'll see you in the morning."

With a short little wave of their hand and a charmingly awkward grin, Hyde returned to the books on the table. Teresa watched them briefly and then made her way outside. She closed the door behind her, making sure it was shut tightly. Hopefully, Hyde or one of the cats would lock up after her.

Teresa took a step forward and froze. She tilted her head to the side while her gaze drifted along the side of the bus. Something definitely wasn't right.

She slipped her hand into her pocket and gripped

her phone while inching closer to her double-decker home. She kept herself from touching anything while inspecting the new scrapes along the door. Someone had pried it open and then shoved it closed. "What the…?"

Before doing a further inspection, Teresa knocked on the front door of the bookshop in the hopes Hyde would answer. She wanted a second pair of eyes to look at it. And she didn't want to be alone in the dark.

"Resa? Everything okay? Mortar and Pestle were quite frantic about getting me to open the door and check on you." Hyde had wisely kept the cats inside the bookshop. They'd pulled on their coat before stepping outside. "What's wrong?"

"Hyde? Give Fynn a call. Someone's tried to force this door open." Teresa stood up from where she'd crouched to inspect the damage and gestured to the side of the bus. "There's loads of scrapes, as if they've used a metal bar or something. Not touching it because there are flecks of it in the paint. And it's making my fingertips itch just being this close for some reason."

"Think we listen to too much true crime while we're knitting?"

"Probably. But that's not why I noticed. I helped refurbish every inch of this bus. I know every tiny bit of damage to the paint. These are new." Teresa hovered her fingers over one of the marks without touching it. "They hacked up my baby trying to get inside."

Hyde eased their phone out of their pocket. "Did you check the windows?"

Muttering a curse, Teresa made a slow circuit around the double-decker bus. She saw a single window had been skilfully removed. The intruder had obviously given up on the door and found a better access point.

"Over here." Teresa nodded to the open window. There was no broken glass on the ground. "I'm thinking they obviously know how to install glass. Maybe a glazier who moonlights as a crook?"

"Or they used magic of some variety. How hard is it to remove one of these?"

"With the right tools? Probably not too hard. But if they could manage this, why not do that to start with? Why try to force the door instead?" Teresa was grateful they hadn't broken the window. She could hopefully get it fixed quickly. "I'm going to see if anything is missing."

"Maybe we should wait." Hyde followed her back around the bus. They almost ran into her when Teresa froze mid-step. "Resa? What's wrong?"

"What do I have of value in the bus?"

"Money?"

Teresa shook her head slowly, and a horrifying thought occurred to her. "I don't keep cash in the bus. And I'd certainly not be the first choice if they were trying to get a lot of cash. I don't do that much business this time of year."

"Then?"

"There's only one thing of value in my bus. My family grimoire. The recipes and rituals? To the right person, they'd be worth a fortune." Teresa felt like cold hands were squeezing her heart. She couldn't breathe, imagining the loss of the one thing connecting her to her mystical lineage. It grounded her despite their having no interest in being in her life. "Bollocks. I'm not waiting for Fynn."

"What about fingerprints?"

"I've touched every inch of this bus just about. My prints are already there." Teresa rushed forward, scrambling to get the door pushed open. She had to know if the grimoire was gone. She stumbled up the step inside the bus. "I have to know."

"Easy." Hyde helped her get to her feet. "Hurting yourself won't help."

Taking a moment to breathe and try to calm herself enough to function, Teresa clambered up the few steps inside. She attempted to ignore the sense of doom and rapid fluttering in her chest. Nothing seemed to help.

"Easy." Hyde followed her into the bus. They guided her to one of the small stools to help her sit down. "Can you tell me three things you see right now?"

"I…." Teresa rubbed a hand over her chest, forcing herself to remember how to breathe deeply. "I see the pan in the sink that I left to soak. I see a jar of cinnamon I didn't put away. And I see the faintest freckles on your cheek."

"Okay." Hyde patiently waited while Teresa took a shuddering breath. "What are three sounds you can hear?"

"My heart is pounding in my ears," Teresa whispered. She closed her eyes for a moment and tried to listen. "I can hear an owl. And I hear some of the wolves howling in the distance."

"Good, good. Can you move three of your body parts?" Hyde prompted after a few seconds of quiet in the bus. "Resa?"

Teresa brought her hand up and wiggled her fingers. She rolled her head from side to side, feeling the tightness in her chest begin to loosen. "Where'd you learn the three-three-three method for helping with an anxiety attack?"

"I asked Hamish the other day when he came in

to pick up his book order." Hyde stepped back to give Teresa a little room. "He said it was a simple trick that might help."

Hamish Keir, one of the local druids who happened to be an EMT, was a friendly bloke. He often popped by the truck for tacos in the middle of his shifts. Teresa had learned a lot from him on coping with anxiety, something he also dealt with.

"Thank you." Teresa reached out to give Hyde's hand a squeeze. "I have to see if they found the grimoire."

"Give yourself a second."

"I can't. I'm not going to be able to settle until I know if it's gone." Teresa pulled herself up to her feet. She'd staved off the anxiety attack with Hyde's help, but her mind refused to stop spiralling over the grimoire. "Will you keep an eye out for the police?"

"Of course."

To her immense relief, Hyde didn't press to follow her, not that Teresa expected them to do so. The vampire was remarkably adept at knowing when to back off. Maybe it came from years and years of having to gently remind others about their own boundaries.

Teresa crept cautiously up the narrow stairs to the upper deck of the bus. Everything was a mess. It was as if the intruder had shoved everything to the floor.

All of the drawers and cabinet doors had been opened. They'd made a thorough inspection of her home. "Bollocks."

"Everything all right?" Hyde called from downstairs.

"It's a complete mess." She carefully tiptoed through the maze of her belongings, trying to avoid damaging anything further. She knelt down to the hidden cubbyhole underneath her bed and prayed to the goddess for a little luck. "Please. *Please.*"

Gathering up her courage, Teresa shoved aside the shoeboxes. She breathed a tentative sigh of relief when the lock appeared intact. She quickly undid it and opened the cubbyhole. The grimoire was inside, still wrapped in ritual-blessed silk.

"It's safe," Teresa yelled down to Hyde. She wiped away grateful tears, sinking back on her heels and closing her eyes for a moment. "They didn't find it."

After a few moments, Teresa replaced the grimoire in its hiding spot. She climbed to her feet and carefully retraced her steps through the wreckage. It was going to take ages to clean up the mess.

Hyde had retreated outside the bus, waiting for one of the police to show up. "Fynn messaged me. He's on his way, hopefully without his boss."

"They were definitely searching for something. I

can only imagine it was my grimoire. Nothing's missing. And it's the only item of value I own." Teresa wrapped her arms around herself, trying to ease the trembling in her hands. Shock and relief were warring in her mind. "I can't believe this happened. I've never had anything like this. The village is usually so safe."

"And now we've had a murder and a break-in." Hyde rubbed their hands together while shifting back and forth. "Weird coincidence. Someone tries to steal your family grimoire when mine was anonymously sent to me."

"A very odd coincidence." Teresa wasn't sure she believed in coincidences. "And right at the time one of my coven leaders was murdered."

"Why don't we pop inside and warm up? I'll make up a fresh pot of tea for us. Fynn might want some." Hyde hesitated by the bookshop door, waiting to see how Teresa responded. "Or I can do that while you stay here."

"I can't understand how we didn't hear anything." Teresa shook her head. She dragged her fingers roughly through her hair, shoving it back out of her face. "How did…?"

Hyde fidgeted for a second before stepping back over to Teresa. "I had the music going. It probably masked any of the sounds. They didn't break the glass. And the damage to the door is minimal. I'd wager they stopped when they realised how much effort it would take to get it open."

"What if they'd found the grimoire? I'd never have gotten it back."

Hyde placed a hand tentatively on Teresa's arm. "But they didn't. It's safe. And the damage to your bus is easily repaired."

"You're very calm."

"I'm very good with other people's crises. Terrible with my own." Hyde turned their head towards the right. "Ready for our second police inquiry? Fynn'll be here shortly."

"I wasn't ready for the first." Teresa chuckled weakly.

9

HYDE

Fynn strolled towards them with one of the constable twins beside him. There was, thankfully, no sign of the chief inspector. Hyde didn't have the emotional energy to deal with him again. "I messaged Aadil. He was on his way home from the wake at the pub. He promised to grab his tools and swing by to fix your window."

Aadil Fadel was a djinn who ran the local garage and happened to be a skilled glazier as well. Hyde knew him because he'd helped with the stained glass in the shop. He also popped by to chat with them about ancient Egyptian scrolls and habitually taught the cats BSL, or British Sign Language.

While Teresa showed Fynn and Constable Trishna Jain the damage inside the bus, Hyde remained outside. They didn't enjoy being cramped into a

small place with multiple people. Instead, they considered how the break-in had happened without anyone hearing.

The glass hadn't shattered, so removing the window had been done expertly and quietly. But the attempt to force the door open would surely have made some noise. Hyde had rather sensitive hearing, and even the music playing shouldn't have drowned everything out.

And where had they gone after potentially failing to steal the grimoire?

Family grimoires were closely guarded secrets for the most part. Hyde had never asked for details about what Teresa's might contain. They couldn't help wondering what might be worth the risk of being caught in the burglary attempt, if that was what they were after. It seemed a safe assumption.

Deciding to explore a little, Hyde walked down Harbour Lane. They went in one direction for a minute or two, then retraced their steps to go the same distance in the other. Nothing stood out to them. There was no sign of the intruder.

Hyde went to turn around when something caught their eye in the darkness. They continued forward until they reached the side of The Woolly Witch.

A prybar had been discarded in the small alley.

Hyde pulled the sleeve of their cardigan down to pick it up. They inspected it carefully, giving the metal a quick sniff.

Iron.

It was not something usually found in the village, as so many inhabitants had an allergy to it. Hyde didn't think it was a coincidence that they'd found an iron prybar abandoned so close to the scene of the crime. It also explained why Teresa's fingers had been sensitive to being close to the flecks in the paint.

Placing the prybar back where they'd found it, Hyde took a quick photo with their phone before sending a text message to Fynn. He immediately responded with a note not to touch anything. They decided not to mention having picked it up.

As Hyde waited, a familiar van pulled up beside them. Aadil waved from inside. He lowered the window. Hyde needed a minute to process what he was signing to them. They weren't as fluent as others in the village.

"I was walking." Hyde spoke and signed at the same time. Aadil was more adept at lip reading than Hyde was at signing. Though, he'd told them in the past that reading lips wasn't ever a guarantee. He gave them a bemused but suspicious look, as though he didn't fully believe the answer. "Okay, I was seeing if I could locate anything indicating where the burglar went."

"And?" Aadil signed. "Did you see anything?"

"I found an iron prybar." Hyde gestured to the item on the ground. "Fynn should be all right touching it, but Constable Jain and Teresa will both want to avoid it. And I'm guessing you will as well."

Aadil immediately nodded. He gestured towards the bus in the distance. "I had a spare window from when we repaired the broken glass after the storm the year before last, so hopefully, I can replace it without any issues."

After signing a goodbye in reply to his, Hyde watched him drive off down the lane. Fynn passed him on the way. He had a large paper evidence bag in hand to secure the prybar. Once he had, he handed it off to Trishna, who smiled before wandering back towards the bus.

"What made you think it was suspicious?" Fynn continued his close inspection of the little alley. He paid close attention to the walls and the ground. "It could've just been left by Magali."

"Magali?" Hyde frowned. They hated it when Fynn tried to draw them into a puzzle. It was so hard to tell if he was making fun or not, though he'd never done so in the past. It still confused them. "Magali, who happens to be a witch?"

"As indicated by the name of her yarn shop—The Woolly Witch."

"Magali's a born witch. Not one for religious purposes. She'd never touch iron. It'd give her the worst sort of rash. Maybe not as dramatic as if Luce came near it." Hyde shuddered to think what might happen to the lone village fae if they'd come in contact with the prybar. "If I'm right—"

"And I definitely believe you are," Fynn interrupted, turning in their direction and almost blinding them with his torch. "Sorry."

"Anyway, if I'm right, why use an iron prybar? It had to be a conscious decision, didn't it? In our village? Our county? Who'd even have iron?" Hyde remembered decades ago when there'd even been talk of making it an illegal substance. A teenage Battista had almost died after accidentally coming in contact with a wrought-iron gate. "Someone brought it on purpose. But why? Was it magically enhanced to make breaking into the bus easier?"

"It didn't succeed if so. They had to go in through the window." Fynn was at the end of the alley. He inspected the locked gate. "No signs of tampering with this."

"Fynn."

"Hmm?" He lifted his head, once again shining the torch in their direction. "What is it?"

"What if they thought it might disrupt any protections placed on the bus?" Hyde knew most villagers had some form of magical defence on their properties. It was part and parcel of living in a mystical community. "Can you tell if it's cold iron?"

"I'm sure a blacksmith might be able to tell. I believe it's considered stronger than wrought iron. I'm not sure."

"I should've licked it."

"Pardon?" Fynn finished looking at the gate and retraced his steps to them. "Licked it? I'm almost afraid to ask why."

"Cold iron is made by hammering it without heat, right? I imagine it tastes different."

"Hyde."

"Hmm?" Hyde blinked a few times. They'd been lost in thought, trying to figure out how they could test the theory. "What?"

"You're not licking my evidence."

"Fine." Hyde sighed. They still remembered what the metal smelled like. It might be worth tracking down smelted iron to see if there was a difference. "I won't lick your evidence."

Fynn coughed a few times before motioning for them to join him as he walked back towards the bus. "I might suggest the chief inspector give it a try."

"Fynn. He already hates me. Please don't make it

worse." Hyde was both horrified and amused at the idea. "Take a picture if he does, though, will you?"

"I wouldn't dare." Fynn patted their arm comfortingly. "Are you doing all right? It's been a rather chaotic evening for you."

"Not just for me." Hyde stopped walking. They wrapped their arms around themselves, staring off into the distance. "Teresa had a panic attack. I helped her calm down."

"That's a good thing. You helping, I mean. Not the attack itself." Fynn waited patiently for them to continue. "Hyde?"

"Does the chief inspector really hate me?"

Fynn seemed momentarily surprised by the question. He shook his head after considering it briefly. "Frustrated, I think, is the more appropriate word for his feelings. I do believe he genuinely wanted to help you settle into village life. He takes his responsibility as the eldest vampire in Scotland seriously. I'm no mind-reader."

"Seer," Hyde coughed.

"Hmm. Yes, I am a seer, but you and I both know it doesn't work quite like everyone assumes. More to the point, I don't *see* him having any bad intentions towards you or any vampire within his coven's domain." Fynn added a dramatic inflexion to the last word. He grinned when Hyde reluctantly chuckled. "Why the question?"

"There's something about the grimoires." Hyde didn't know what specifically, but it bothered them enough to push through the discomfort to speak to DCI Pacheco. "Maybe he'll be able to answer my questions."

"Or leave you with more questions."

"Or leave me with more." Hyde sighed. "You're supposed to help me feel better, not worse."

"I'll go with you when you ask. How's that?"

"Marginally better." Hyde rubbed their eyes tiredly. They felt grimy and gritty. "I need some sleep."

"In your coffin?" Fynn teased.

Hyde shoved him into the lane.

"Careful. DCI Pacheco might arrest you for assaulting one of his detectives." Fynn continued walking beside them. "It's going to be okay, Hyde."

"Not even you can see that for certain."

10

TERESA

Constable Jain had finished with all the crime scene photos. She'd made short work of getting fingerprints off a few surfaces. Teresa had been too lost in thought to pay attention to the magic used.

Sitting on the bench in front of the bookshop, Teresa stared glumly at her pride and joy. She'd put so much effort into renovating the old double-decker. There was a sense of violation at having her home intruded upon.

"Ms Vega."

Teresa frowned at DCI Pacheco, who'd slipped up on her without her noticing. "Yes?"

"Tell me about your grimoire."

"No," she hissed instantly.

He immediately raised his hands, attempting to

put her at ease. "I've no interest in your family secrets."

"Such as they are." Teresa lowered herself back onto the bench, forcing herself to take slow, deep breaths. "What are you really asking me?"

"Without giving me any specifics, is there anything in your family grimoire worth stealing? Would someone who isn't connected to the Vegas have a reason to attempt to take it?" He crouched down so he was no longer looming over her. "South Myrddin is a quiet village. We've rarely seen crime here in all of the centuries I've been here."

"And now there's been a murder and an attempted burglary. Or potentially been one. I don't know for sure what they wanted, but the grimoire is all I have worth stealing."

"Exactly. I don't believe in coincidences." He pulled a notebook from his coat pocket. Teresa struggled to keep herself from smiling. It felt like something right out of one of the true-crime mysteries she'd read. "Why go after your grimoire? You're not the only person in the village with one. They targeted you specifically."

"I don't...." Teresa struggled to answer his question. She'd been trying to figure it out since she'd noticed the break-in herself. "My abuela Lucia always told me to keep it safe. She was quite insistent. I never expected this to happen, though."

DCI Pacheco frowned at her response. He stared off into the distance for a moment before returning his attention to Teresa. "I'd suggest you read through it from cover to cover. In my experience, there are many family secrets hidden in the pages of grimoires. And I've seen people die to protect theirs. I'd prefer to keep everyone in the village safe if I can."

Teresa met Pacheco's gaze without flinching. He was a striking man. Tall with what her mother would've called a lithe form. His greenish-brown eyes seemed far too observant. He kept his greying beard and hair immaculately trimmed. It was the haughtiness in his aura that caught her attention the most. "Why do you hate Hyde?"

"I don't hate them." His response was sharp and immediate. He sighed deeply, pinching the bridge of his nose. She had to keep from snickering when she heard him counting backwards in Spanish under his breath. "I would very much like to help Hyde. My intention when they arrived in the village was to welcome them into our coven. Despite my best efforts, they misunderstood me at every turn."

It wasn't his words, Teresa finally realised. Whether intentional or not, his delivery came across like an arrogant teacher who assumed their pupil was too ignorant or lazy to understand. Condescending. Patronising. She could think of several other words to describe his mannerisms, none he'd appreciate hearing.

"Did you ever consider changing your approach?"

"No."

Teresa shook her head at him. She didn't necessarily think DCI Pacheco had bad intentions, but his delivery was never going to work with Hyde. "They're never going to want to be part of a group that reminds them so strongly of the family who abandoned them. And I don't blame them. Have you ever even once attempted to understand them even the slightest?"

"My job—"

"Your job as coven leader is almost parental, particularly to the younger members. Your job is to take care of them. And yet, all I've seen you be is dismissive and patronising." Teresa sniffed derisively. She rubbed her hands together to warm them up. "I don't really have anything else to say to you."

Suddenly exhausted by everything, Teresa walked around the bus to where Aadil was finishing the repair. She leaned against the side and closed her eyes. Thankfully, he didn't seem to mind her presence at all.

Teresa finally opened her eyes after a while. She tapped his shoulder and then attempted to muddle through signing—something she was still learning to do. "Thanks for coming so quickly."

"Anytime." Aadil smiled. He reached over to correct the form of her signing. "Take care of yourself —and of Hyde. They're good people."

With a cheery wave, Aadil packed up his tools and returned to his van. He beeped the horn twice and then drove off. Teresa inspected the repaired window briefly; she'd have to add a little extra tip to the bill for him coming out so early in the morning.

Hyde joined her after a few minutes. They leaned against the bus beside her with a tired groan. "Fynn and His Royal Highness are having important police-type investigations."

Teresa snorted in amusement, managing a some-what weary chuckle. "It's going to take forever to clean up the mess in my bus."

"We'll tackle it after we get some sleep. The mess isn't going anywhere. The locks work. You've got a window. And I doubt the pillock's going to return in the middle of the day." Hyde pulled the sleeves of their cardigan down to cover their hands. They stared up at the sky, which was just starting to show signs of daylight. "I've the pull-out couch. You're welcome to rest on it. The cats won't bother you much."

From the stubborn set of Hyde's jaw, Teresa knew there was no point in arguing. She'd planned to clamber over the mess and sleep in the bus—it wouldn't hurt to suffer through it for one night—but the couch sounded imminently better than being alone.

Teresa didn't comment when Hyde checked the shop lock multiple times before leading her upstairs into their little flat. Mortar and Pestle followed at a leisurely pace. The two cats stretched themselves out in front of the fire and watched them struggle with the couch.

"I swear this was easy the first time I did it." Hyde tugged one last time, falling back when the couch finally shifted. "Balls."

They laughed together. Teresa helped Hyde up to their feet. Between the two of them, they finally managed to get the bed set up correctly.

Mortar jumped onto it, circling before getting comfortable. Pestle trundled sedately towards Hyde's room. The cats had obviously decided to keep an eye on both of them.

"I'll let you have the bath first. Washing the day away might do both of us some good." Hyde wandered over to a cabinet and pulled out a couple of towels. "Here."

If the day had been any less traumatic, Teresa would've laughed at how awkward they were being with each other. She clutched the towels to her chest before reaching out to take Hyde's hand.

"It's going to be okay." Hyde nodded a few times as if to convince themselves, then pulled away and disappeared into their room.

Teresa sat on the edge of the bed once Hyde had trudged off. She collapsed backwards, staring up at the ceiling.

They're not having my family grimoire. I don't give a damn who they are or why they want it.

11

HYDE

A PERSISTENT TAPPING DRAGGED HYDE FROM THE depths of sleep. One of the cats had pulled open the curtain nearest the bed. The sunlight was painfully bright.

The knocking continued, breaking through the fuzziness in her mind. Hyde scrubbed her hands over her face and rolled out of bed. It was going to be a long day. She felt distinctly more feminine today than neutral.

Grabbing the nearest and cleanest pair of trousers and a random jumper, Hyde trudged down the narrow stairs into the shop, being as quiet as possible to avoid waking Teresa. She paused to flip the sign from Shh to Hello and from They to Her. When she opened the door, DCI Pacheco's glaring visage was not a welcoming sight.

"I don't want any." Hyde went to close the door, frowning when he placed his hand on it and pushed it open. "It's too early for you to be this annoying."

Behind her, Mortar and Pestle had both leapt onto the shop counter. They hissed indignantly at the elder vampire. He didn't appear overly impressed by any of them.

"We have things to discuss."

"No, we don't." Hyde folded her arms across her chest and glowered at his chin. "There's a proper wake for Florence later today. I don't need you messing with my morning and making it so I don't have the energy to attend."

"I'm not the enemy."

Hyde wasn't entirely certain about that, but she could admit he didn't intend harm towards her. "Please go away."

DCI Pacheco hesitated before finally withdrawing his hand from the door. "Perhaps after the wake, we can speak."

Without answering one way or the other, Hyde slowly but firmly closed the door in his face. She locked it and resisted the urge to stick her tongue out. It was a childish impulse that struck her every time DCI Pacheco was particularly annoying.

"Is he gone?" Teresa poked her head into the

shop. Her long brown hair was all over the place. "I was coming down to chase him off."

"Already gone. Mortar and Pestle did a fine job hissing up a storm at him." Hyde plucked both cats up into her arms. They snuggled against her before the former clambered up to perch on her shoulder. "Did you get the text from Emrys? They're setting up the ritual circle at Raven Park to do a proper wake for Florence."

Raven Park was nestled between the loch and a row of cottages along Druid Lane, a small area that mostly served as the official village public ritual circle. The witches' coven and many of the druids used it. Hyde had never personally had a reason to spend time near it.

It was saturated with magic. Village histories claimed Myrddin had anchored protections there because of strong ley lines running through the area. Hyde didn't know enough to say for certain. All she knew was it had a unique smell and always made her feel as though static electricity bubbled up around her.

"Will you be all right?" Teresa stepped fully into the shop. She hadn't changed out of her pyjamas. Her gaze drifted over to the signs on the counter. "Ah. A change for today?"

"A little." Hyde shrugged. "I'm fine. I won't allow

him to wreck my morning. I wish he'd leave me alone. I don't want to be a member of the supersecret fang club."

Teresa choked on a laugh. She broke into hysterical giggles, grabbing the counter for support. "Please. Please let me be in the room when you call it that to his face."

"Resa."

"It would be glorious." Teresa hopped up to sit on the counter. She dragged her fingers through her hair, wincing when they caught on tangles. "I'm a mess. When is the wake starting? I had my phone on silent, so I missed the message."

"Emrys and Hamish lit the bonfires at first light. I believe your coven intends to spend the entire day keeping it going." Hyde wasn't in the witches' coven group chat. Florence had kept her up with the gossip. "I'll be in and out throughout the day. I'll give you a hand cleaning up the bus."

"Let me get dressed. We can grab something from The Golden Puff or Roasted and Toasted for brekkie." Teresa slipped off the counter. She ran her hands across Mortar's and Pestle's heads, then brushed the softest kiss on Hyde's cheek. "See you in a few."

Standing in the middle of the shop for longer than she'd ever want to admit, Hyde finally shook herself out of a daze. She definitely didn't reach up to touch her cheek like a soppy fool. Her cats followed her upstairs to her tiny flat, both appearing bemused by her antics.

What do I wear to a wake?

Something warm?

Hyde prepared herself for the comments about vampires not being affected by temperatures. She didn't care. Sometimes, it was impossible to ignore the slightest of chills from cold winds.

I feel what I feel.

Dithering in front of her closet, Hyde settled on dark brown tweed trousers and a navy blue knitted jumper over a white button-up with the sleeves rolled up. She grabbed a vintage flat cap hanging off a hook beside her wardrobe. It had been a gift from Florence, along with the jumper, which had embroidered vines along the hems. What more fitting way to celebrate her life than wearing things she'd given?

Hyde made sure the cats had everything they'd need. She'd bring them down to the park to say their goodbyes later.

I'm not ready for this.

The previous night had been a blur. Hyde had been too overwhelmed by the mass of noise and people to register the beginnings of grief. All of her attention had gone to managing the stress that came with teetering on the cliff of sensory overload.

Today would be different. She hoped. It couldn't be worse.

Though the skies hadn't cleared, Hyde thought the gloomy clouds were more appropriate. She didn't feel joyful.

When Hyde arrived at the park, she immediately spotted Florence's two partners, who'd come with every intention of celebrating their friend's life.

Flossie and Winifred had worn their brightest outfits. They sat together, smoking from elaborately carved pipes, ones Hyde thought Florence had gotten for the three of them on one of her trips. The third had been set on the empty chair between them.

Making her way over to them, Hyde managed a smile. She thought it might've come out more like a grimace. Flossie reached out to take her hand and patted it gently.

Hyde tried to find the words. "I miss her."

"She's not really gone, poppet. She'll find ways to make us laugh even now." Flossie released her hand. She puffed on her pipe and blew out a few impressive smoke rings. "Didn't the boys do lovely work with the fire?"

"Go and say hello. Leave us to our smoke and memories." Winifred waved her off. She leaned into Flossie. The two smiled and began whispering to each other. "Off with you, poppet. We're not going anywhere."

Leaving the two witches to their pipes, Hyde wandered around the other side of the massive bonfire. She stayed outside the circle etched into the sand. Vampires and rituals didn't always mix well together; she didn't want to risk ruining anything by accident.

Hyde glanced back to find Teresa in deep conversation with Magali, one of the other members of her coven. She continued on until she found Hamish and Emrys contemplating their work. The two greeted her cheerfully as always, though it was understandably a tad muted from their usual vibrance.

In Hyde's limited experience, druids tended to be dramatic and overtly cheerful. There were no shrinking violets amongst the ones she'd met. Bright and airy, attuned to the world around them, there always seemed to be a hint of otherworldliness about them.

"Be careful, foundling." Emrys's gaze drifted over her head to the fire behind her. His eyes seemed utterly unfocused. He grabbed Hamish's shoulders when he swayed on his feet. "We care for our own."

Without giving her a chance to respond, Emrys spun around and vanished from sight. Hyde stared at the space where he'd stood before turning to

Hamish. His hand was still held up where he'd been supporting his fellow druid.

"We're not all as gifted or dramatic as Emrys. Or as old." Hamish shook his head. "He's been grumbling about something he's seen coming for days."

Hyde shivered as icy fingers of fear danced up her spine. "Am I in danger?"

"We protect our own." Hamish patted her on the shoulder and then stalked away.

"That's not comforting." Hyde sighed when he simply lifted his hand and waved without even glancing back in her direction. "Overdramatic foresty berks."

Leaving Teresa to speak with her coven, Hyde found herself heading down Harbour Road from the park until she reached Druid Lane. It was a short walk before she stood before Florence's cottage. Police tape was still stretched across the front like a massive "X marks the spot."

There were no words to soothe the tightness in her chest. Hyde missed Florence. It had been so disconcerting to see Flossie and Winifred alone together without her.

"Did you know her?"

Hyde almost jumped out of her skin. She had no idea how she hadn't heard the man approach.

"Everyone in the village knew Florence—and not just because she led the coven of witches."

"Aye. She made sure everyone knew her." He stepped closer to where she stood at the gate.

It took all of her self-control not to take a giant step away from the man. There was something menacing about him.

He was older, maybe in his late sixties or early seventies. He had a full head of grey hair with flecks of black here and there. His blue eyes were cold as ice and hard as steel. His face seemed permanently set into a glowering frown, practically etched out of granite.

Hyde got the feeling he expected some sort of response, though she had no idea what since he hadn't asked a question. "Why are you here?"

His frown immediately deepened, so that had clearly not been what he'd expected. "I'm Angus Peck."

"Good for you."

"Florence was the love of my life." Angus's face tightened when he said the words.

"Was she? Were those feelings reciprocated?" Hyde caught the scent of something familiar when he took another step closer. She tilted her head to the side, trying to subtly sniff out what it was. "You're a warlock."

"Druid."

"No. They smell earthy, like a freshly tilled garden mixed with moss and wildflowers. They're nature personified like a brisk breeze through the woods on a spring morning." Hyde didn't describe how a warlock differed from a druid in scent, not out loud to the man. She didn't want to insult him by commenting on his dank, muddy rottenness, dark and heavy like the undergrowth of an ancient forest where poisonous mushrooms grew. "You're a warlock."

"I *am* a druid." He emphasised the word as though it was a title.

It wasn't.

"No, you aren't." Hyde did take a step back when the air around him seemed to crackle with energy. "Hamish is a druid. So is Emrys. They don't smell like you."

Warlocks, in general, tended to avoid South Myrddin. Hyde didn't know the ins and outs of why. There was something in the village that made it an unpleasant place for them.

"Emrys?" Angus went very still.

"Yes. Him. He's a friend." Hyde had every intention of kicking the old druid in the shins the next time she saw him. He needed to get better at his warnings, since he'd failed to mention the creepy warlock who'd pop out unexpectedly and attempt to ruin her morning. "Why are you here and not at her wake? If Florence was the love of your life? Was she aware of holding that title?"

"Mx Snodgrass. What have I said about staying away from crime scenes?"

Despite the icy tone in DCI Pacheco's voice, Hyde had never been more grateful to hear it. She side-stepped away from Angus and retreated to a safer distance. The elder vampire seemed utterly unim-pressed.

"You haven't technically said anything." Hyde glanced between the two men before shrugging to herself. "I'll just be heading back to the wake."

"Mx Snodgrass." DCI Pacheco hesitated before finally waving her off. He turned his full attention to Angus. "And who are you?"

12

TERESA

It had taken a moment for Teresa to realise Hyde had wandered off. She'd gotten drawn into conversations with some of the coven members about what happened next since Florence would no longer be there to lead them. No one was quite ready to use the words "replace her," but it would eventually become necessary.

As a newer member, Teresa rarely felt comfortable offering her opinions. Anxiety probably didn't help. Her chest tightened whenever someone began pointedly asking who she felt was up to the task.

When Hyde strolled quickly back into the park, Teresa was relieved and concerned. Her vampire friend had very nearly been running, which was not something she was prone to do. Something had definitely happened.

Teresa excused herself from yet another conversation about Florence's passing and weaved through other groups of mourners to reach Hyde. "Has something happened?"

Hyde latched on to Teresa's wrist, pulling her with impressive speed towards the group of druids gathered at the edge of the ritual space. "I'll tell you in a second. I need to ask Emrys a question."

"Okay." Teresa allowed herself to be dragged along. She enjoyed the strength of Hyde's grasp on her arm. "I think he's finally finished with ensuring the fire remains for the duration of the wake."

Hyde marched up to the druids. She finally released Teresa's arm, glancing down as if surprised that she'd been holding it. "Angus Peck."

"Ah." Emrys rubbed his beard absently as though he were some stereotypical ancient mage from a cartoon instead of one of the most powerful druids in Scotland. "You may want to ask Flossie and Winifred. They'd know more about Florence's former paramours."

"Paramour? Who even…? No, I will not be distracted." Hyde shook her head. She fidgeted absently with the ring on her finger, spinning it in one direction and then the other. "You said 'ah' like you knew the name."

"A warlock of dubious reputation." Hamish

inserted himself into the conversation when Emrys stared absently into the fire.

"Is there a good one out there?" Teresa responded when it became clear Hyde and Emrys were engaged in a bizarre staring competition. The latter gazed absently into the fire while the former glared at the side of his head. "Think we can get these two back into this discussion?"

"Give them a moment. Emrys has to commune with nothing. It adds to his mystique." Wilfred, one of the other druids and the village doctor, winked at Teresa when Emrys muttered to himself. "I'm aware you can hear me. But until you deign to behave yourself, I'll continue to poke holes in the bloated balloon of your ego. It's good for you. Keeps your feet relatively close to the ground."

"Tell me about Angus Peck. You wouldn't be all...." Hyde waved her hand around, clearly hunting for a word and not finding one. "You wouldn't be all *you* if you didn't know something."

"You were correct about their having a certain reputation, generally speaking. But Angus Peck is more than just your average warlock. He is rotten to the core. I wouldn't trust him within a hundred kilometres of the village." Emrys reached a hand out towards Hyde. He didn't touch her, just held it inches from her chest, closing his eyes and muttering under his breath in a language Teresa couldn't understand. "He is obsessive. Possessive. He's dangerous."

"He was also standing outside Florence's cottage." Hyde had frozen in place when Emrys began chanting. She didn't move until he finally lowered his hand. "He claimed to be a druid, but I didn't believe him. Smelled wrong."

"Smelled wrong?" Wilfred piped up from where he'd gotten distracted by adjusting the fire. "How so?"

"Well, maybe not wrong for a warlock. He smelled like rotten compost." Hyde began fidgeting under the intense gaze of all three druids. Teresa slipped over to stand beside her, looping her arm around the vampire, who relaxed a little. "You're earthy like the forest in autumn after a storm."

"Fascinating." Emrys looked as though he had a thousand questions he wanted to ask but wisely restrained himself. He stepped back, drawing his fellow druids with him, which gave Hyde some much-needed space. "Maybe he came for the wake. I imagine he kept track of Florence over the years."

"Or maybe he was here for an entirely different reason." Hyde glanced over her shoulder at the bonfire. "I'm going to pay my respects, then go to the bookshop. I've had enough excitement for one morning."

They said their goodbyes to the druids, then made their way through the throng of mourners. Teresa had already offered her ritual chant for the dead. She stood sentry beside Hyde, making sure no one bothered her, even if just for a friendly chat.

Whatever had happened with Angus, it had clearly unnerved Hyde. Teresa waited patiently while the vampire at her side remained silent in front of the fire. It was almost a full ten minutes before she moved.

"Ready?" Teresa asked. She smiled when Hyde looped her arm around hers. They turned to leave, only to stop when someone blocked their path. "Lonnie."

"Vega." Lonnie Batch hadn't been in the village in over five years. Florence's estranged nephew had fled after being caught stealing from his aunt's pub. He was a jack of all trades but certainly a master of none. "Vampire."

"Wastrel." Hyde had been the one to catch Lonnie. He'd never forgiven her for outing him to his aunt. "What are you doing here? Didn't Florence disown you?"

"We were reconciling." Lonnie had grown up in the village. He'd run around the pub like he owned it as a teenager. "I had tea with her a few times this past month."

"Did you?" Teresa found it strange that Florence hadn't mentioned it at their knitting group. She usually gossiped about everything happening around the village. "She never said."

"Flossie and Winifred reacted badly when Auntie Florence mentioned putting me back into her will." Lonnie dropped his voice down to a whisper, leaning in closer to them. "They tried to force her to sell her third share of the pub back to them. They didn't want to risk me having a say in the running of the place."

"Did they?" Teresa wasn't inclined to believe him, but she couldn't help remembering how tense things had been between the three witches. "Florence told you? Why would she trust you after everything you did?"

"We're family."

Teresa raised her eyebrows at the response. Maybe for the rest of the world that might engender an immediate trust, but the people of South Myrddin were painfully acquainted with how blood relations could turn on someone for no reason at all. "That doesn't mean much of anything. We were Florence's family. The coven. The village. You were a thief who took advantage of her."

"I was doing better. She was *my* aunt. This is my heritage." Lonnie had gotten loud enough that the rest of the mourners were starting to notice. "It's mine. No one can take that away from me. Not you. Not those two old bints. Not even Auntie Florence."

"When was the last time you saw your auntie Florence?" Hyde played with the ring on her finger, spinning it back and forth. She stared intently at Lonnie's hands, though Teresa wasn't sure why. "Did you have tea with her this week?"

"I did. Why?" Lonnie's eyes narrowed suspiciously. He leaned in closer to them, causing Hyde to rear back. "Are you accusing me of something? You—"

"Think it's time you moved on, mate. Don't you?" Rees Mohan came up behind them. He dropped a large hand on Lonnie's shoulder. "You're not disrupting the mourning today. Off with you."

Lonnie spun around to argue, only to stumble away from Rees, who towered over him. "Fine."

It didn't appear fine. Lonnie muttered every curse under the sun at them while storming through the crowd. Teresa was relieved to see him go, not wanting to draw such negativity into the coven's ritual of remembrance.

"You all right, little duck?" Rees checked Hyde over carefully.

Hyde sighed at the nickname. "One time. One time, I tried to help a duck. I was a child."

"You followed it around like a lost duckling for a

month. Poor shifter didn't know how to change back and not break your heart." Rees roared with laughter when Hyde smacked him on the arm. "Have you eaten? I've got the Malt Moon open, so swing by if you want the little duck special."

Once Rees had moved on, Teresa and Hyde continued their way out of the park. Thankfully, they didn't run into any further trouble. It was a relief to finally make it back to the bookshop and taco bus, even if there was a massive mess to clean up.

"You have the oddest relationship with the people in the village." Teresa had come here later in life than most. Hyde had grown up in South Myrddin. "What's the little duck special?"

"Battered blutwurst and twice-cooked chips."

"Blutwurst?"

"German blood sausage. They're dipped in beer batter and fried. Surprisingly delicious. And I like my chips twice-cooked sometimes. Extra crispy." Hyde unlocked the door and let her cats out to explore. "Rees always enjoys exploring what he can do in his fish and chip shop."

"Little duck?"

"I was very young. I didn't understand there could be more than one kind of shifter. And it was an adorable duck. I thought it needed help getting back to the loch, which, in retrospect, is silly." Hyde crouched down to pick Mortar up and hide her face against the cat's fur. "Why don't we start cleaning up the bus?"

"Hyde?"

"Hmm?" She lifted her head to glance towards Teresa.

"Could Lonnie have killed Florence?"

Hyde sighed deeply. She rested her chin on top of Mortar's purring head. "If he thought it might gain him an inheritance? He just might."

"We should tell Fynn." Teresa didn't want to run into DCI Pacheco again. "He'll be more likely to listen to us."

"He's going to be so obnoxious." Hyde sighed. She set Mortar down and retrieved her phone. "He always thinks I'd make a great investigator. I have the nose for it."

"Well, you did sniff out the pecker."

"I haven't sniffed any sort of pecker. Ever. I identified a warlock." Hyde snorted. She glowered when Teresa snickered again. "Don't. You know, speaking of sniffing out...."

"Yes?" Teresa stopped her inspection of the damage on the outside of the bus and turned her full attention to Hyde. "What did you smell?"

"On Lonnie. Something floral and sickeningly sweet. It was the same undertones I noticed in

Florence's cottage when we found her." Hyde finished whatever message she was sending to Fynn. "It could be a coincidence."

"But you don't think so?"

"No. No, I don't." Hyde gripped her phone tightly. "But I also don't want to believe he'd murder his own auntie."

Teresa opened the door to the bus. She peered inside at the mess the intruder had made of the business part of her home. The kitchen was a disaster. "This is going to take forever."

"We'll manage. Is anything broken?"

"My heart?" Teresa tried to laugh, but it stuck in her throat. She was so proud of the bus. She'd worked so incredibly hard to buy it and renovate it. "I'll fix it."

Hyde patted her on the back a little uncomfortably. "We'll do it together."

13

HYDE

Step one of cleaning up the bus involved more manual labour. Hyde dragged one of the large bins behind the bookshop over to the door. It allowed them to easily toss the unfixable things.

Bent pans, broken dishes, and all manner of ruined paper products were dumped unceremoniously into the rubbish. They'd turned on music to fill the awful silence. Hyde could see the toll all of it had taken on Teresa.

After an hour of clearing out the unfixable items, Teresa slumped onto one of the seats in the corner. She covered her face with her hands and screamed in frustration. Hyde carefully made her way through the bus, sitting on a turned-over box and placing a hopefully comforting hand on the witch's shoulder.

"Sorry."

"Scream again if it'll help." Hyde shrugged. She wasn't the best at offering comfort. "Why don't we take a break? Grab something to eat? Or, at least, a strong coffee? Think it might be good for you to step outside the bus for a few minutes."

"Let's stop by Roasted and Toasted. Maybe Shikoba has something special to go with our coffee," Teresa encouraged. "The fresh air will do us both some good. They've always got a few treats to share."

They walked up Harbour Road past Selkie Street until they reached the coffee shop. Shikoba Apanni had come to Scotland from Louisiana as a young person. They were part of the Choctaw nation, a two-spirited eagle shifter who'd opened Roasted and Toasted a few years earlier. It was one of Hyde's favourite places in the village.

"Hyde," Shikoba greeted when they entered the shop. "Who are we this morning?"

"A tired she." Hyde slumped against the counter dramatically. "We've had quite an adventure."

"So, I'm thinking strong coffees, maybe with the salted caramel sauce. And you're in luck. I've got chocolate spiced cake fresh out of the oven." Shikoba immediately got to work on their drinks. "I heard about the break-in at Guac-a-mole. Are you all right?"

"Been better." Teresa sat on one of the bar stools at the counter. "It could've been worse. They didn't steal anything; they just messed up the place."

There was a pleasant peace to Roasted and Toasted. It likely came from Shikoba. By nature, they seemed to exude calm in a way Hyde greatly envied.

The eagle shifter had a quiet strength to them. Their long inky-black hair always reminded Hyde of a raven's feathers. Shikoba had black eyes and more tattoos than Teresa, which was impressive in and of itself.

"What has you both rattled this morning? Aside from a murder and a break-in?" Shikoba set two mugs on the counter. They made the art of coffee seem almost like alchemy. "I thought I saw Lonnie Batch sneaking around. Wasn't he banned from the village?"

"Strongly warned about returning, but not exactly excommunicated officially." Teresa perked up when Shikoba served up extra-large slices of the cake. "He...."

Hyde glanced at Teresa when she failed to finish her thought. "He said a few things we found concerning."

"'Calling the police' concerning?"

"I texted Fynn. Does that count?" Hyde gratefully accepted the mug of coffee. The scent alone did wonders for her mood. "He promised to keep an eye out at the ritual wake."

"Ah, yes. I'll be by late this evening when the embers are low for my goodbyes." They patted Hyde on the shoulder. "Ask her. She won't say no."

Hyde could only sigh as Shikoba wandered off to help another customer. There were rarely secrets in a village with multiple seers. She sighed, then turned to find Teresa watching her intently. "We've got more cleaning to do, but can I take you out for dinner?"

"I'd love to." Teresa's immediate answer eased Hyde's nerves. Maybe it was a good thing she'd been nudged into asking. "How about Al Dente or Wok Away?"

"Wok Away. We're less likely to have the entire village watching us like some drama on the telly." Hyde felt like someone had shaken a bottle of champagne and opened it in her stomach. She shook her hands out at her sides, trying to dispel some of the energy. "Rees is due to practise with Mortar and Pestle tonight, so they won't be alone. And he can keep an eye out for the intruder."

"Is he still convinced they'll be a blues trio with him?"

"They do meow when he plays his guitar." Hyde greatly enjoyed watching Mortar and Pestle with Rees. They'd sit mesmerised while he played his guitar, punctuating the music with sounds of their own. "I'm not entirely convinced they weren't bards in a previous life."

Teresa scowled at her briefly before they both dissolved into helpless laughter. "How have I never seen this?"

"No idea. They don't do it often." Hyde finished her coffee not long after Teresa, and they said their thanks to Shikoba and headed out of the coffee shop. "What's the plan?"

"I need to make a list of things to order for the bus. And then cleaning. We've thrown out all the ruined things. The kitchen, especially, has to be cleared up and sanitised before I can even think about cooking." Teresa stared tiredly down the lane. She kicked a stray pebble in the street, launching it up into the air and watching it crash to the ground. "A pity I can't wave my hands and magic it all away."

"I think our magic is going to require more manual labour than fancy words." Hyde knew it would take a while before Teresa felt comfortable in the bus. A break-in was a violation of the sanctity of her personal space. Her castle. "I'll help."

Teresa reached down to grab her hand. She held it while they continued walking. "Thank you."

They cleaned for another hour before Hyde had

to return to the bookshop. It was a while before Fynn stepped into the shop, just as she was preparing to close up early for her date. She frowned at the seer, wondering if something had happened with Florence's case.

"Do you have a moment?" he asked.

"Is this about a book or your murder inquiry?" Hyde waved him over to the counter. She smiled when he paused to pick up Pestle, who had rubbed against his leg.

"The latter, unfortunately. I'd rather chat about books with you." Fynn gently set Pestle on the counter, though he continued to pet the cat. "DI Filippov and DCI Pacheco are following up with Angus Peck. I don't do well around warlocks. Their aura is jagged and sharp. It's like the physical manifestation of a migraine."

Hyde leaned across the counter and dropped her voice to a whisper. "Do you call them DI and DCI when you're at the police station as well?"

"Hyde." Fynn sighed tiredly. "No, I don't. I call DCI Filippov, Nastia. And DCI Pacheco, boss or Jonatan. Also, they aren't here. They can't hear you."

"With my luck? They'd definitely hear. Interesting." Hyde didn't know that it was, actually, but she'd found it always better to attempt at being polite. She'd learned the hard way over her decades on Earth that people could be quite sensitive. "So, what are you here to ask me about?"

"Lonnie Batch."

"Ah, the prodigal son—or nephew, I suppose. The heir apparent, according to him." Hyde sat on the stool behind the counter. She was already exhausted by the day and hoping for a break. It would be humiliating to spend the entire date yawning. "Florence never mentioned she'd reconciled with him, which surprises me."

Fynn flipped through his notebook, pausing on one of the pages. "You were the one to catch him stealing from the pub?"

"I was. There wasn't a massive inquiry into it. But he was run out of the village."

He held his hand out towards her. "May I?"

"Fine." Hyde rolled her eyes but placed her hand in his. He covered it with his other one and closed his eyes.

This feels so unnecessary.

There was a long silence in the bookshop. Mortar and Pestle sat at the end of the counter, watching them intently. Fynn remained still, not doing anything aside from clutching her hand loosely between his own.

Though a gifted seer, Fynn rarely attempted to gaze

so directly into someone's future. He'd once told Hyde about a few nightmares from his youth when he'd had little control over his skills. It was a delicate business, being able to describe both the good and bad to come.

"Promise me you'll be careful over the next few days." Fynn set her hand down on the counter, lightly patting it before pulling back. "It's all muddled, but the sense of danger hasn't passed."

"I'm always cautious. Overly so, according to most." Hyde glanced up when the door opened, setting off the little bell. "Hello, Rees. No chips?"

"I figured you wouldn't want to eat before you go." Rees joined them at the counter. "I'm here with my guitar to entertain the kittens while you have your date."

"I'm sorry, what?" Fynn glanced between Hyde and Rees. "What's happening?"

"They like to listen to the guitar and meow." Hyde shrugged. Fynn stared at her in confusion. "What? And he likes to practise."

"Not the mongrel and the kittens. Nothing he does surprises me. What's this about a date?" Fynn brushed off Rees's playful growl. "Did Teresa finally ask you out?"

"I asked her."

"Our little duck is all grown up." Rees easily

caught the ball of string Hyde threw at him. "Violence is never the answer."

"Says the werewolf who hunts in the forest at least once a month." Hyde returned the ball of string underneath the counter. She glanced over at Fynn. "Was there anything else? I need to get ready for my date."

Fynn shook his head. "Not at the moment. If I have any questions, I'm sure they can wait until tomorrow. Just—"

"Be careful? I will."

Hyde darted upstairs, leaving the cats with Rees. She stood in front of her wardrobe and eyed up her varied collection of clothes. "What do I even wear on a first date?"

14

TERESA

THE UPSTAIRS OF THE BUS HAD THANKFULLY BEEN MORE straightforward to clean up. Less had been broken in the upper levels, so Teresa was able to get away with simply putting things back into place. It allowed her to have plenty of time to prepare for their date.

Once Hyde had left for the bookshop, Teresa called Wok Away. Evelyn Tham promised to have a private table set up for them near the back. It would hopefully allow them some semblance of a regular first date.

There was bound to be loads of gossip about their having dinner together as an official date. Nothing stayed secret in a small village, particularly one like South Myrddin. And especially when one of the people involved was Hyde, who everyone adored.

Hyde had an almost magical ability to draw

people to herself. Maybe it was the way she openly accepted everyone for the most part. Morrigan had once mentioned how the vampire had a pure aura that attracted both good and bad.

It was the latter that had almost the entire village looking out for Hyde. She could take care of herself, but there was also a hint of naivety that drew her into trouble.

Pushing those thoughts away, Teresa scrounged through her closet for something to wear. The majority of her wardrobe contained a variety of graphic T-shirts and a host of jeans. She found a nice pair of black denim and a shirt Hyde had gifted her for Yule. Wok Away wasn't the fanciest of restaurants, and Teresa had never been one for dressing up, but she wanted to look nice for the date.

She dithered in front of a mirror after showering and getting changed, trying to decide what to do with her hair. The distraction was welcome after a mentally and emotionally draining day of cleaning the bus. Teresa brushed her hair out quickly, deciding to leave it down.

A quiet tapping on the glass let her know Hyde was waiting downstairs.

Throwing on her leather jacket, Teresa raced down the steps. She hopped over a box on the floor and went out to meet Hyde. They stood awkwardly in front of each other for a second, both unsure of what to do next.

Though it surprised both of them, Hyde made the first move. She stepped forward and softly kissed Teresa's cheek. With a glare at the whistling from inside the bookshop, she held her arm up for the witch to take.

"Remind me to find a dog toy for Rees," Hyde grumbled.

"Maybe some kibble?" Teresa knew the werewolf would find it funny. She slipped her arm out of Hyde's and reached down to take her hand instead. "You dressed up for me."

Hyde peered down at her outfit. "Did I?"

Teresa stretched her hand out to pick a ginger cat hair off Hyde's blazer. "If I'm not mistaken, you've worn your favourite cardigan. The special occasion one."

"Resa."

She almost felt bad for just throwing on a pair of jeans and a T-shirt, even if the latter had some sentimental connection to their budding relationship. "I'm almost underdressed."

"You're not." Hyde immediately shook her head. "I love your hair like this."

"Wildly untamed?"

Hyde hesitantly ran her fingers through the ends

of Teresa's hair. She couldn't help shivering pleasantly at the touch. "It's silky smooth and adds to the air of motorcycle kitchen witch."

"Motorcycle kitchen witch?" Teresa snorted. She'd never really labelled herself as other members of the coven did. "I like it. I've certainly got the tattoos and devil-may-care attitude to pull it off."

"Is it really devil-may-care if you call yourself that?" Hyde continued on down the street, seeming oblivious to the villagers who'd spotted them holding hands. Teresa had no doubts gossip would be flowing all evening about their date. "Want to know a secret?"

"Anything you'll tell me."

"I was intimidated by you when you first arrived." Hyde leaned in closer. Their arms pressed together as they buffeted each other from the wind that had picked up on their walk to the restaurant. "You were wild and untamed. Tattoos and leather jackets. You made magic with food. And you were like a goddess from one of my books. Beautiful and clever."

Teresa didn't quite know how to take this vision of herself from Hyde's perspective. It was humbling and also mildly terrifying. "You're adorably sweet."

"That's me. I'm just a ginger marshmallow."

"So, what you're saying is you're the deliciously

soft and sweet marshmallow, and I'm the slightly spicy yet decadent chocolate in our hot chocolate?" Teresa burst out laughing when Hyde shoved her away. "What? I'm enjoying the metaphor."

"Resa—" Hyde was cut off by an ominous cracking sound. "Did you hear that?"

Teresa paused and threw herself at Hyde, knocking both of them into the lane. She covered the vampire with her body and tried to roll them further away from the falling tree. "Bollocks."

Despite her best efforts, Teresa only managed to move them a short distance. The mighty oak crashed down around them. Thankfully, they'd narrowly avoided being struck by the trunk. The smaller limbs still bashed into them, though.

"Are you two all right?" Magali had popped out of her yarn shop at the sound of the tree falling. "Don't move."

"Hyde?" Teresa had been thrown a little by the tree falling. She couldn't see Hyde's face. "Are you all right?"

"Been better." Hyde's voice was muffled but strong. She managed to shift her arm to brush her fingertips against Teresa's side in acknowledgement. "You?"

"It's odd. A tree falling for no reason at all. Solid oak. I imagine it's been around for centuries, given how big it was." Teresa assessed her injuries quickly. Nothing appeared to be broken, but she had no doubts there would be plenty of bruises and scrapes. They were trapped in a prison of tree limbs, branches, and autumn leaves. She wiggled slightly and found it difficult, but not impossible, to move. "Think I can make my way out of this. Can you head in my direction?"

"Maybe," Hyde grunted. "Balls."

"Hyde?" Teresa tried with some difficulty to twist her head to the left for a glimpse of her. "You okay?"

"Tree limb in the ear. Not pleasant. I don't recommend it."

With the help of several werewolves and one of the village dryads, they managed to extract themselves without doing more damage to themselves or the poor old oak. Teresa glanced over at Hyde, who had scratches and bruises on her face and arms where her sleeves had gotten shoved up. She imagined her own body was similarly marked.

"What's happened?" DCI Pacheco's sharp voice made both Hyde and Teresa groan. She wondered if he'd been in the village to continue the murder inquiry. "Has someone called the ambulance?"

"I'm fine," Hyde hissed.

There was a flash of emotion across Pacheco's face that Teresa noticed. It was gone before she could analyse it further. He shook his head and turned away from them.

"Hyde?" Teresa placed a hand lightly on her shoulder, not wanting to aggravate any unseen bruises. "Think he was just trying to do his job."

"I know." Hyde leaned into her with a tired sigh. "It's almost instinctual at this point. He's a sore spot. No matter how lightly it's touched, it's still going to hurt."

Teresa nodded in understanding. She knew exactly what it was like to have someone who'd caused such aggravation that it still triggered a bad reaction no matter how they changed. "Not sure what we're going to do for a second date, because this is already the most memorable one I've ever had."

After a prolonged silence, Hyde began to snicker. It took only a moment before they were both laughing hysterically. All of the stress and strain faded away in the absurdity of it all.

Even with DCI Pacheco glowering at them, it was several minutes before they managed to pull themselves together. He'd called in Constable Vitya Antonov, another local shifter, who took Teresa's statement about what had happened.

"I'm not sure how helpful this will be. All I heard was an ominous crack, and then the bloody tree fell on us." Teresa peered around him to where DCI Pacheco was speaking to Hyde. "Maybe we should—"

"We should let them figure this out one way or the other." Vitya shook his head. He tapped his pen against his notebook. "Any thoughts on who'd want to do this?"

"It wasn't an accident?"

"I took a glance at the trunk. Someone definitely took an axe to it." Vitya dashed her unrealistic hopes of it simply being an accident.

"Well, bollocks."

15

HYDE

HYDE SHOVED HER HANDS INTO HER BLAZER POCKETS. IT was getting colder and windier. Her hopes of enjoying her favourite dim sum while on an official first date had been dashed by a weathered old oak tree. "I can't tell you anything."

"Mx Snodgrass." DCI Pacheco seemed as if he'd prefer to be anywhere other than asking her questions. She could definitely relate. "Just walk me through what you remember leading up to the tree falling."

"I don't remember."

"Try." He was doing an admirable job of restraining himself from snapping. "Any little detail can help."

"I was holding Teresa's hand." Hyde closed her eyes in the hopes that not seeing him would make it

less irritating and embarrassing. "We were walking to Wok Away. I don't remember what we talked about."

"And then?"

"I...." Hyde held a hand up to stop when he went to prompt her again. She mentally went through each second of the walk, trying to pull the memory back from where it had gotten distorted by the chaos and stress. "I heard this sound. It was almost like a shotgun. A loud crack. The rest is a blur. I think Teresa lunged at me. She sent us flying into the street."

"Did you see anyone by the tree?"

"I didn't even see the tree until the branches were poking me in the ear." Hyde finally opened her eyes. She gripped her dusty and ripped hat in her hands. One of their rescuers had found it for her. "We were just going on a date. I didn't ask for the old oak to fall on me."

"Mx... Hyde." DCI Pacheco took a step towards her. He placed a surprisingly gentle hand over hers. "Please be careful. Someone has clearly decided either you or Ms Vega is a threat."

"You don't like me," Hyde stated confidently.

"I don't dislike you."

Hyde frowned. She didn't grasp how those were two different things. "Feels the same."

"I'm consistently frustrated by how you never

seem to react how I expect." He was being far more candid than she could ever recall him being. It kept her from making a snappy comment in response. "I acknowledge this isn't fair to you."

Hyde pushed aside her knee-jerk reaction to brush it off like it was nothing. "I can't possibly be the only autistic vampire in the world. I'm not a unicorn."

"Agreed."

"Perhaps you could educate yourself instead of trampling all over our differences and expecting everyone to react the same way." Hyde toyed with one of the rips in her hat. "I'm never going to respond the way you expect. I can't. I don't even realise most of the time that I've done something 'unusual' by your standards."

"The coven has rules. All covens have rules."

"And yours don't make sense to me." Hyde clenched her hands around the hat. She didn't think they were ever going to be able to find some kind of middle ground. And if she were honest with herself, she didn't really care. "Are we finished? I'd really like to be anywhere but here."

"Hyde?" Teresa sidled up beside her. "I've answered all of Vitya's questions. Why don't we head to the bakery? Maybe Rosa'll have something to warm us up. We can decide if we still want dim sum while we're there."

A sharp whistle drew all of their attention. They finally spotted Rosa at the door of The Golden Puff. She glowered at her uncle before motioning for Hyde and Teresa to head her way.

"Are we finished, Detective Chief Inspector?" Hyde stared at the fallen oak. They'd dragged the poor thing off to one side. "If you have any more questions, I'm sure you can find us."

They quickly made their way across the street to the sanctuary of Rosa's bakery. Hyde noticed Ada Senft walking towards the fallen tree. She was a dryad who ran an orchard on the outskirts of the village and was also skilled in woodcraft.

"I hope Ada turns the oak into something beautiful. Poor old tree." Teresa looped her arm through Hyde's as they continued on to the bakery. "I'm sorry about our date."

"It's certainly been memorable." Hyde managed a smile at Rosa, who bustled them inside and firmly closed the door. She glared one last time at her uncle before turning to the two of them. "I think he was genuinely attempting to be kind. Or, at least, his version of it."

"How odd. I wonder if he strained a muscle in the process. It is very much against the Pacheco nature.

I'm an anomaly." Rosa guided them over to the little round table at the back of the bakery. It was mostly a grab-and-go shop with only a small seating area. "How about I whip something up to warm you? The wind is biting out there. I've got a new blend for you to try. It's a ginger spiced hot chocolate. Oh, and here's my first aid kit. Why don't you take care of your scratches? None of them look serious."

Hyde glanced over at Teresa, who pressed her lips together, bringing her hand up to her mouth. "Ginger spiced hot chocolate?"

"What are you two giggling about? Are you in shock?" Rosa frowned worriedly when they dissolved into laughter. "Honestly, what's going on?"

"Sorry, sorry." Teresa was the one to pull herself together first. She opened the first aid kit and began checking Hyde out. "Just a joke we'd made before the catastrophe with the tree."

"Right." Rosa glanced between the two of them. She frowned for a moment before shrugging and heading behind the counter. "Was that a yes?"

"It's definitely a yes. I'm all about hot chocolate. I love a sweet and spicy ginger." Teresa ignored the embarrassed huff from Hyde. "I'll send a text to the Thams. I don't want them to think we're blowing off our reservation."

"I'm sure they noticed the massive tree crashing

into the lane. Why don't you see if they'll put together a takeaway for you? Let you continue the date in the safety and familiarity of the bookshop." Rosa busied herself behind the counter. She nodded at the plate she'd set near them. "I've some of my wonky-shaped chocolate orange croissants. The first batch tasted perfect but went a little wrong."

"I'm sure they're delicious." Hyde immediately grabbed one of the misshapen pastries. It appeared to be an attempt at something loosely orange-like. In one of the display cabinets, she could see a better version. "Those look brilliant. How'd you manage it?"

"Skill and creatively cursing my ancestors." Rosa winked at them before returning her attention to the hot chocolate. "Did he say anything about who cut the tree?"

"Nope. Vitya didn't know. I did overhear mutterings about it; obviously, it's been cut. How'd they manage that without anyone noticing? Definitely very odd." Teresa finished her croissant fairly quickly. "Think they're regretting not having more cameras in the village."

"Hard to have them when people kept ruining them accidentally." Hyde took another bite of her croissant.

"Accidentally on purpose." Rosa snickered. "He

ranted about it quite a bit a few years ago when they tried fitting the village with them. He doesn't buy the excuse that certain technology doesn't mesh well with the levels of magic around us."

"Hard to disagree when my laptop works, as do our phones. No reason the CCTV cameras wouldn't either." Hyde licked a stray bit of chocolate off her thumb. She glanced towards the door to the street beyond it. "It would've certainly made figuring out who killed Florence easier. Not to mention who broke into the taco bus and tried to smash us with a grand old oak tree."

"Here you go, darlings. Enjoy." Rosa set two mugs on the counter in front of them. "Someone has to have seen something."

"My question is this: Are we dealing with separate incidents?" Hyde got to her feet and wandered over to the door with the hot chocolate in hand. She watched Vitya, DCI Pacheco, and Fynn stand around the fallen tree. "Is the attempted burglary connected to Florence's murder? And who felled the oak?"

"Maybe the burglary and tree were done by the same person? They both involved Teresa," Rosa pointed out. She crouched down to adjust the bread in one of the display cabinets.

"True. How does the murder fit in? Or does it?" Teresa finished the last of her croissant before taking a sip of the hot chocolate. "Feels like the murder is unrelated."

"That's actually more frightening than them being connected. Two or more people wreaking havoc in the village as opposed to one person." Hyde leaned in closer to the glass with her nose practically pressed against it. "Why's Lonnie hiding in the alley?"

"Hmm? I can't tell for sure. It's not light enough out. We don't all have your brilliant sight." Teresa sidled up next to her with Rosa close behind. They all peered at the figure partially hidden in the shadows between the post office and One Crafty Dimension. "It certainly looks like him. Odd."

Grabbing the phone behind the counter, Rosa began dialling. Hyde kept her gaze on the figure in the shadows while listening to her friend speaking to someone. She had a feeling, based on the pure curtness in her voice, that it was her uncle.

Rosa usually had an almost pathological need for politeness and warmth. Hyde always wondered if it was why she'd opened a bakery. Soft, cosy, and kind. But much like with herself, Jonatan Pacheco brought out the worst in his niece.

Hyde frowned when she spotted one of the constables and Fynn heading towards the alley. Lonnie, or whoever it was, backed away slowly before taking off at a run with the police in pursuit. "I hope they catch him. Bit odd, him standing there watching from the shadows."

"Like a thief? Or a criminal returning to watch the aftermath of the destruction they caused?" Rosa stepped up behind them. "My uncle thanked us for our help and politely asked us to remain out of the investigation."

"Politely?"

"I shall choose to interpret his general boorish behaviour as a confused sort of civility." Rosa spoke in a disturbing imitation of DCI Pacheco at his worst. She grinned mischievously at them. "It's not as if you've gone hunting for suspects."

Hyde shifted a little guiltily beside Teresa. "We were researching types of poisons."

"Nothing wrong with a little research." Rosa leaned in closer to them, lowering her voice. "What books were you using? Maybe I can make some suggestions."

16

TERESA

AFTER PICKING UP THEIR TAKEAWAY DIM SUM, THEY made their way back to the bookshop. Mortar and Pestle were happy to see them. Hyde got the fire going upstairs after seeing Rees off, and they sat on the rug with their food on the coffee table.

Teresa watched in concern as Hyde became more and more withdrawn. She'd definitely hit sensory overload. "Why don't I leave you to rest? I still have cleaning up to do in the bus. And you look absolutely done in."

With a slight shrug and a nod, Hyde dragged a blanket off the armchair behind her. She wrapped it around herself. Mortar and Pestle immediately plastered themselves against her.

"I see you're in good hands." Teresa gathered up

the remnants of their dinner. "I'll clean this up and check in on you later."

Part of her wanted to end the evening with a kiss, but Teresa knew it was ill-advised. She didn't want to add to the overwhelm. Hyde managed a weak wave as she left, closing the door as gently as possible.

The bookshop was eerily quiet in the darkness. Teresa couldn't help checking in all the shadowy corners before leaving. She didn't want to risk anyone trying to go after Hyde.

After making sure the door was locked behind her, Teresa crossed the distance to her bus. She frowned when she noticed someone loitering towards the back. Her suspicions were immediately aroused when the man swiftly backed out of view.

"Oi." Teresa jogged towards the back of the bus. She caught sight of the man fleeing down the lane, and she picked up the pace. "Come back here."

Racing after the man, Teresa caught up to him just as he rounded a corner and tried to vanish behind a shop. She found herself face to face with a suspiciously twitchy Lonnie Batch. The angry glint in his eyes made her regret going after him alone.

Teresa opted to bluster her way out of the situation. "Why the devil were you skulking around my bus?"

"I wasn't."

"You were. Why else would you run?" Teresa folded her arms across her chest. She glowered at the man, who seemed to be losing his courage by the second. "Now, colour me suspicious, but I've had my bus broken into, and your auntie's been murdered. So, why were you spying on me? Or in the book-shop? Or both?"

"I have no idea what you're going on about." Lonnie scowled at her. His eyes kept darting around as if hoping for a distraction or someone to intervene. "Who wouldn't run away from someone screaming at them?"

"Why were you there?" Teresa repeated her question, pressing him for an honest answer.

"Just shut up." Lonnie clenched his fists at his sides, cursing her under his breath. "I haven't done anything to your sodding bus. I wasn't there for you. I don't give a rat's arse about you. I was—"

"Who were you there for?" Teresa took a step towards him. "Hyde?"

The air around them crackled with energy. Teresa muttered a protective chant, relishing in the familiar warm embrace of her family ritual. She held her ground when he practically growled at her.

"You interfering bint." Lonnie launched himself at her.

The second his hand touched her, the protective

magic sent him flying. He scrambled to his feet and fled before she could stop him. Teresa was left alone in the alley with adrenaline coursing through her.

Teresa leaned against the wall to her left as the energy slipped away. She breathed in through her nose and out through her mouth. Her hands shook uncontrollably as anxiety rushed in to fill the gap where her courage had been. "What was I thinking?"

"Teresa?"

Teresa smothered down the urge to scream. She acknowledged Trishna with a weak wave. "I'm fine, Constable Jain."

"Teresa? I'm off duty. Tell me what happened." Trishna came around to stand in front of her, gently taking her by the wrist and placing two fingers over her pulse. "It's a beautiful night, eh? What colour would you say the sky is?"

Teresa found herself staring up at the partially cloudy sky. "Indigo? That's a colour, right?"

Her mind whirred with the names of colours. She continued to list them to Trishna. Somehow, in the midst of analysing the precise shade of night, she found her breathing beginning to even out.

Teresa leaned her head back against the wall and finally took a deep breath without the tightness in her chest. "I'm all right."

"If you say so. Why don't we get you back to your

bus? I've given my sister a text. She's patrolling this evening. We'll all keep an eye out for Lonnie." Trishna shook her head sadly. "He's always been trouble, but I'd hate to think he had something to do with his own auntie's murder."

Teresa could only shrug in response. She'd seen family do terrible things to one another. It was part of what had caused the village to be founded, after all. "I'm not saying he had something to do with her death, but he was definitely hanging around the bus. I'm not eager for another break-in."

"We'll have a not-so-friendly chat." Trishna reached out to steady Teresa when she wavered on her feet. "You okay?"

"Fine, fine." Teresa ran shaky fingers through her hair. She waved off Trishna's concern. "I'm good. Think I'll head home, though. I've suddenly had more than enough fresh air for one day."

Trishna grinned at her. "I'll walk you back to your bus—make sure Lonnie's gone for good."

17

HYDE

When Hyde woke up the following morning, it occurred to them that they'd neglected one potential source of information. The family grimoire was hidden downstairs in the bookshop. They hadn't checked it for the poisonous plants.

It was distinctly a *they* sort of day. Hyde closed one side of their wardrobe and opened the other. They quickly dressed, fed the cats, and rushed into the shop, curious to see if the grimoire would hold the answers.

Mortar and Pestle followed them down the stairs into the bookshop. The former headed towards the door while the latter stayed close to their side. Hyde was hyper-focused on getting the grimoire; they had to find answers.

Hyde logically knew it wasn't their job, but they

couldn't shake the fear from the day before. The tree could easily have killed them. They'd both been lucky to escape with a few bruises and scrapes. "What do you think, Pestle? Will we find answers?"

A curious mewl caught her attention from the direction of the door. Hyde set the grimoire on the counter and went to investigate. Pestle joined them.

"What've you found?" Hyde found Mortar sitting near the front door with a paw resting on a bakery box. It had The Golden Puff's label on it. "Has Rosa sent us a breakfast treat? Did you let her in?"

Lifting the box, Hyde opened it to find one of their favourite pastries from the shop. Rosa had obviously decided they needed a little pick-me-up. They grabbed their phone to invite Teresa to join them, pausing to flip over the She sign to They.

While waiting for Teresa, Hyde perused the family grimoire. It was less a collection of spells and more of a family history along with bits of information their ancestors had found useful. One entire section was dedicated to poisons, so they started there.

"I found it. I think this is what killed Florence. It was right here all along." Hyde tilted the grimoire so Mortar and Pestle could sniff at it. "And it's one of the rarer plants that I'm immune to. It'd just make me really sick. I had no idea vampires were unaffected by certain poisons."

The cats seemed entirely unimpressed by the discovery. They were more interested in the pastries. Hyde took a bite, ignoring the plaintive looks sent their way.

Hyde deftly deflected the reaching paws when a knock sounded on the door. "It's open."

"Morning." Teresa's gaze darted over to the sign on the counter, then back to Hyde. She continued over to peer into the box. "Oh. Rosa sent pastries?"

"There's plenty—" Hyde bent over and clutched at their belly. "Oh, gods above. Or maybe below."

"Hyde? What's wrong?"

"I don't know. I've had a couple pastries and nothing else. Maybe I'm allergic?" Hyde fought against a wave of nausea. They absolutely loathed being sick. "Maybe Rosa didn't send them. Oh. Resa? I don't… I think something's wrong. Very, very, very wrong."

Teresa lunged forward to catch Hyde when their knees went weak. "Easy. I've got you. I'm calling for help."

"I'll be fine."

"You were poisoned."

"We don't know that for certain." Hyde thought about what they'd read in the grimoire. If they had been poisoned, the killer might not know vampires were relatively immune. "Okay, maybe, but it's not going to kill me. I'm just going to be very, very ill. Perhaps point me in a direction away from the books?"

"Hyde? Hyde." Teresa lowered them to the ground and reached into her pocket to retrieve her phone. "You need help."

"I feel so ill," Hyde groaned. They rolled over onto their side, trying to alleviate the growing pain in their stomach. "I hate being sick."

"I'm texting Wilfred, then calling for an ambulance. He'll get here far quicker." Teresa tapped her fingers furiously against her phone. She grumbled under her breath while clearly waiting for some form of response. "He's on his way with Emrys."

The two druids rushed into the bookshop in a surprisingly short amount of time. They shoved Teresa out of the way and knelt beside Hyde, who moaned in pain yet managed to point toward the box of pastries. Emrys shouted at Teresa to call the police.

"Be nice," Hyde groaned.

"Hush, foundling." Emrys placed a cool hand on their forehead. He muttered Gaelic under his breath. "Wilf? Do you have charcoal on you?"

"Oh. No. I don't want to be sick," Hyde grumbled

weakly, not that it mattered to either of the druids. "Emrys."

"I am sorry, but you'll feel loads better once it's out of you." Wilfred had retrieved a packet of the abominable powder and a bottle of water from his kit. "Better out than in."

"Easy for you to say." Hyde choked down the activated charcoal with a lot of grimacing and grumbling. They managed to get most of it down. "Someone should ask Rosa about the box. I doubt she'd poison me."

"I'll tell Fynn when he arrives," Teresa promised. She was still tapping away on her phone. "Ambulance should be pulling up in a minute or two."

"We're going to transport you to my clinic so I can monitor you while the charcoal works its magic." Wilfred gently helped them to their feet. He looped an arm around their back to offer strength. "Let's get you outside."

"I'll take care of Mortar and Pestle. I'll come see you at the clinic once I'm sure Fynn has everything he needs." Teresa grabbed their hand and gave it a gentle squeeze. She glowered at Wilfred. "Take care of them."

The following hours were as unpleasant as Hyde expected. Wilfred's cheerful "Better out than in" didn't help matters at all. They'd been tempted to chuck something at his head but refrained. He had done everything in his power to make it better.

Teresa arrived after Hyde had finally been able to shower and rinse their mouth numerous times. They felt almost back to normal. "Wilfred said it was safe to come in to see you. I brought your grimoire."

Hyde sipped the warm herbal concoction Emrys had given them and smiled. "I think the worst is over. What did I miss?"

Teresa dragged a chair closer to the bed and took a seat. "They sent the pastries off to be tested. Rosa said a man she didn't recognise bought them, but she gave the police a description. How are you feeling?"

"Better. Don't ask me what Emrys's concoctions did to get me to feel better. You don't want to know." Hyde grimaced. They didn't want to think about it themselves—and they'd been the ones to go through it. "I have to stay here for the night. Wilfred wants to make sure there are no other side effects."

"A wise precaution." Teresa reached out to take their hand. "You scared the life out of me."

"Not literally." Hyde pressed the tips of their fingers to Teresa's wrist. "Strong pulse. Heart seems to be beating just fine."

"Beating for you." Teresa grinned when Hyde blushed and then groaned. "Too cheesy?"

"A mild cheddar level of cheese. Not quite

limburger." Hyde laughed before quieting almost immediately. "My stomach's still sore."

"Sorry." Teresa tightened her grip on Hyde's hand. "Maybe I should kiss it better?"

"My stomach?"

"Not quite." Teresa shifted from the chair to sitting on the edge of the bed. She reached up to run her fingers through Hyde's riot of short ginger curls before dragging her thumb along their jaw. "Can I kiss you?"

Hyde swallowed thickly, unable to find words for a second. "Yes."

It was their first proper kiss. They started out sweet and tentative but fell into each other. An almost desperate sense of trying to confirm they were both still alive and well.

"I do hope I'm not interrupting." DCI Pacheco sounded amused at having caught them. Hyde jolted back from Teresa but kept a hold of her hand. "I wanted to speak to you about your family grimoire. You've read it, haven't you?"

"Why don't I go check on Mortar and Pestle? They've been alone for a while. We wouldn't want them to take it upon themselves to come find you." Teresa leaned in for a light peck on the lips before leaving. She paused by DCI Pacheco. "Be nice."

"Be gone, witch." He glared when she muttered

in Spanish at him. He finally turned his attention back to Hyde. "Did the grimoire hold any other details about the poison aside from it not being deadly to vampires?"

There was a prolonged silence where Hyde stared at the grimoire. Pacheco eventually cleared his throat. He sighed and repeated his question when they looked blankly at him.

"I don't know." Hyde had gotten distracted by the pastries and being ill. "I'll check."

"I—" DCI Pacheco was interrupted by his phone ringing in his pocket. "I'll take this outside."

Alone in the room, Hyde took a few minutes to recover from the kiss and the interruption. Despite the mild discomfort left over from being ill, they felt like they were floating on air. It was magical and wonderful; even the embarrassment of being caught couldn't drag them down.

Raised voices drew their attention. Hyde covered their mouth to keep from laughing. They could just make out Wilfred loudly berating DCI Pacheco for being on his phone in the clinic.

After soaking in the wonderment of their feelings, Hyde reached over to grab the grimoire off the table. They'd never imagined something connected to their family might matter. They'd gone out of their way to avoid them for so many decades.

Hyde thumbed through the grimoire to the page they'd found earlier. A note they'd missed at the bottom caught their attention. "Remains benign until activated by warlock ritual."

Warlock?

Oh… balls.

Angus.

Slamming the grimoire shut, Hyde grabbed their phone. They tried texting Teresa, but she didn't respond. After a moment of hesitation, they called, but again, there was no answer.

"Wilfred? Anyone? Hello?" Hyde shouted for help. They'd been told not to leave the bed since even the druids weren't completely sure how the poison might affect them. "I need help."

"What are you bellowing about?" DCI Pacheco stepped into the room. He frowned when they tried to get out of bed. "What the hell are you doing?"

"I found out more about the plant." Hyde caught DCI Pacheco's attention by practically hitting him in the face with the grimoire. He flipped to the page when they kept insisting. "Only a warlock could've brought out the poisonous qualities."

"Peck."

"Teresa's not answering my calls." Hyde was glad he believed her about the poison, at least. He seemed dubious about the rest.

"I'm sure she's fine."

"Like I was fine after being poisoned or having a tree fall on us?" Hyde refused to allow him to dismiss her worries. "She promised to come back after checking on Mortar and Pestle. She's not answering her phone, and she texts me back right away. Something's wrong."

Emrys stepped into the room, having heard the last part of the conversation. "We'll go check on her."

"We?"

"Would you rather I deal with Angus Peck myself? I'd be more than happy to do so, though I think you'd prefer a more legal method of justice than my own archaic one." Emrys winked at Hyde when Pacheco capitulated in the face of his threat. "I'll make sure Teresa is fine."

Hyde could only nod their thanks. They couldn't shake the feeling something was wrong. "Hurry."

18

TERESA

With Hyde settled at the clinic, Teresa jogged back to check on Mortar and Pestle. The cats tried to cling to her when she went to leave after filling their food and water dishes. She had no doubts they knew something wasn't right.

Teresa crouched down and lightly ran her fingers over their heads. "They're going to be okay. Dr Wilfred wants to keep an eye on them for the rest of the day, but I'm sure they'll be home soon."

A plaintive meow tugged at her heart. Teresa sat on the rug by the front door. The two cats immediately snuggled into her lap.

"Poor kittens. Hyde will be back. I promise. I don't think Dr Wilfred would appreciate you two being in his clinic." Teresa spent a few minutes cuddling Mortar and Pestle. She eventually eased

them out of her lap and got to her feet. "All right. I've got to check on my bus, then get back to the clinic."

After one last look at the cats, Teresa left the bookshop. Paranoid about someone trying to break in, she made sure to lock up carefully. She turned around and gasped in surprise when a glowering man loomed over her.

"Can I help you?" Teresa tried to step to the side, wanting to put some space between them. She hadn't heard him approach. There was something familiar about him. Her nose wasn't as sensitive as Hyde's, but she caught a faint whiff off him. She had a distinct feeling this was the warlock. "The shop is closed."

"I was looking for the vampire."

"There's several in the village. Could you be more specific?" Teresa edged to the left, trying to put space between herself and the glowering warlock. "I can message Detective Chief Inspector Pacheco for you. He's a vampire. I'm sure he'd be thrilled to answer any questions you have."

A massive stretch of the truth, but Teresa had no doubts DCI Pacheco was up to the task of dealing with Angus Peck.

His gaze darted around as if searching for someone. He lunged forward seconds later to grab her by the jacket, dragging her behind the bookshop where he'd parked his car.

Teresa struggled against the surprisingly strong man. She didn't think she'd be able to scare him off as she had with Lonnie. "Quit yanking me around. What are you even doing?"

There was an awful silence where the air around her seemed to boil with anger. Angus flung her back against the brick wall. She groaned at the impact but managed to remain on her feet.

"What does she know? The vampire? She knows something," Angus hissed almost to himself. He lunged for her again, but she darted to the side. His fingers slipped on her arm. "I just have a few questions for you."

"I have some for you. Why'd you try to steal my family grimoire?"

"What?" Angus frowned at her. He reached out again, but she pulled away. "I won't hurt you."

"Like you did with the tree? And is that what you told Florence before you poisoned her?" Teresa knew she'd hit the truth when he visibly flinched at the words. His eyes narrowed, and his mood seemed to darken. It was like a storm cloud settling around his shoulders. "Why would you kill her? Did she reject you?"

"I adored Florence. You wouldn't understand.

Young people like you. You cannot comprehend the depths of my devotion. I'd have crawled through the abyss of Hades for her. I did." Angus took a step towards her. She backed up only to find a brick wall behind her. The only exit was in front of her. "The vampire won't mourn you. Not like I weep for my witch."

"She wasn't yours. Never was. You had to kill her, didn't you? Were you hoping to…?" Teresa frowned. She remembered Winnie once telling the coven to be wary of warlocks because they often tried to capture the essence of a person, even in death. "She was stronger than you even in death, wasn't she? Did you fail to grasp onto the remnants of her spirit? That why you were outside her cottage? A desperate attempt by a frail man."

"Be silent." Angus clenched his fists at his sides.

The magic crackled around her, so different from her own or the druids'. It was malicious. The weight of it struck her in the chest, and she gasped for air almost immediately.

Her heart beat erratically. Teresa grabbed at the collar of her shirt, trying desperately to ease the pressure. Angus sneered malevolently at her. The invisible band around her tightened even further.

"You were told to leave *my* people alone." Emrys

seemed to appear out of nowhere. "You were warned."

All of a sudden, Teresa found the ominous weight gone. She could breathe deeply. The heaviness in the air vanished as if it had never been there.

There were other voices, but she heard nothing. The pounding of her heart blocked everything out. She closed her eyes briefly, trying to put space between herself and the sudden chaos.

Teresa dropped to the ground. Her legs didn't seem to want to hold her up. She stared blankly at Emrys when he crouched in front of her. "I'm okay."

"Aye. You will be." Emrys held his hand above her head while murmuring in Gaelic. She felt almost light-headed with relief as the jittery sensation dissipated. "You did well."

"I didn't do anything," Teresa argued. She'd barely managed to stay on her feet throughout the confrontation. Several of the police had arrived; they were restraining Angus, but she couldn't hear what they were saying to him. "I'd bet my life he killed Florence."

"You almost did." Emrys patted her gently on the shoulder. "Let's get you over to the clinic. I'm sure Hyde will be worrying themselves sick."

The weight of Angus Peck's glare stuck with Teresa well after they were out of sight.

Emrys walked with her to the clinic. Hyde had definitely been waiting anxiously for news; they didn't calm down until they had a hold of Teresa's hand.

"I'm fine."

"You almost weren't," Hyde stated firmly. "You have the smell of warlock around you—like a deadly floating cloud."

"She's going to be just fine, as are you." Emrys gave both of their hands a squeeze. "I'm going to check the village and make sure Angus didn't leave any unpleasant surprises. Take care of each other."

After a little insistence from Hyde, Teresa managed to cuddle up with them on the clinic bed. They held each other tightly. Her heart finally settled back into a calm pace. She no longer felt like her entire body wanted to vibrate into outer space.

"I don't think he broke into my bus," Teresa said after they'd lain in silence for a while. "He was genuinely confused when I mentioned it."

"Maybe Lonnie?"

"But why? Why would he want my grimoire?" Teresa couldn't shake the feeling they'd missed something. "It's a family one. Personal. There are no coven secrets within, which is the only reason I can think of for him to want it. If he wants to claim any part of his auntie's estate, he's going to need a strong legal case."

"From your family grimoire?"

"I didn't say he was being logical." Teresa lifted her head when the door opened, and Wilfred stepped inside. "Is Hyde going to live?"

"They're going to be fine." Wilfred walked over to where they were snuggled together. He held his hand over Teresa's forehead, murmuring to himself in a similar manner to Emrys. "And so will you. Try not to fall out of bed, will you? And yes, Hyde, I was only joking."

Hyde settled back once Wilfred had left them alone. "Does this count as our second date?"

"I really hope we can do better than a cramped bed in the clinic that has just the faintest whiff of herbs and medical cleansers. Food, at the very least, should be involved." Teresa could think of a hundred different places to have a second date.

"I have crisps." Wilfred poked his head back into the room. "And biscuits."

Hyde snorted with laughter when Teresa launched one of the magazines off the nearby table at him. "Thank you, Wilfred. You are, as ever, always helpful."

"I'll make tea."

"Please go away." Teresa buried her face in Hyde's neck, trying to control her own laughter. It was bordering on hysterical. She allowed some of the fear and tension to bleed out of her. "Crisps and biscuits?"

"We've eaten worse in the knitting group."

"Not even close to the point." Teresa closed her eyes and enjoyed the sound of Hyde snickering. "We'll call this 'second date adjacent.'"

"I'm glad you're okay." Hyde's fingers gripped Teresa's hoodie. "Nothing about my world would be right without you in it."

"Are you done being disgustingly adorable? I've had an idea." Wilfred opened the door and wheeled in a second bed. He lowered the rails and eased it up beside the one they were on. "Best I can do. Let me lock the wheels so you don't go for a ride."

"Wilfred." Teresa narrowed her eyes at the mischievous tone in his voice. She shook her head when he chuckled. "Thank you."

19

HYDE

Samhain was one of Hyde's favourite days of the year. The village turned into something straight out of a storybook or movie. Even with the upheaval of the past few weeks, they were looking forward to what was to come.

The annual Samhain festival started after five. Hyde intended to meander around the village while Teresa had her taco bus open. And then later, the two were going on a midnight picnic by the loch.

It had been a little over two weeks since Angus Peck had admitted to murdering Florence. He'd never confessed to a motive, though he had pled guilty, wanting to forgo a trial. Fynn had confided in Hyde that he thought the warlock wanted to avoid implicating himself in anything further.

All Hyde cared about was the man would never

be able to hurt anyone ever again. Emrys had ensured the prison cell was warded against any potential escape attempts of a magical sort. He'd taken it quite personally when one of his foundlings had been attacked.

They were never able to confirm if Angus had caused the tree to fall. And he'd insisted he'd never been interested in Teresa's grimoire. Both mysteries were unsolved, which left Hyde uneasy.

The weather turned colder. The days shortened. Hyde enjoyed each brisk morning, often taking a walk with Teresa before opening the bookshop. The terrifying adventure had brought the two of them closer together than she thought they might've had the courage to be without a little nudge from abject fear.

With Emrys and Flossie's help, Hyde had created a little memorial in the bookshop. They'd used her favourite chair in the knitting corner. It now sat on the wall between two of the shelves, and a never-dying flame flickered above a cauldron filled with flowers and herbs from Florence's cottage garden. It would remain until they'd said their goodbyes around the Samhain bonfire.

Hyde sighed when the door opened. They'd planned to close up early to enjoy the festival. The man who stepped into the shop made them groan internally. "Lonnie. What are you doing here? I thought you were told to leave the village—again."

"You stole my inheritance." Lonnie stomped towards her, kicking the door shut behind him. "I know you did. This is all your fault."

"Stop stomping your feet like a toddler." Hyde was grateful they had the counter between them. "What are you talking about? What inheritance? Florence left some books to me. Nothing more. Winnie and Flossie have the pub, as they should. And I have no idea what's happened with the cottage."

"You did. I know you did. Just like you ruined everything the last time."

"The last time? When you were stealing from your auntie? All on your own, without anyone helping you." Hyde rolled their eyes at the ridiculousness of the petulant man in front of them. "Have you ever taken responsibility for anything in your life?"

"I know there's something in her grimoire."

"It was you." Hyde had assumed, based on Angus's genuine confusion, that he hadn't tried to steal Teresa's grimoire. He'd have no motive, but Lonnie appeared to have plenty, if only in his own mind. "You broke into the bus."

"I wasn't going to steal anything. I had to check to

see if Auntie Florence had hidden her will." Lonnie's gaze darted around the room. He focused back on Hyde, glowering at them even more intensely. "She had to have left something behind."

"How many grimoires have you checked?" Hyde had heard a few conversations around the village of coven members finding things in their cottages disturbed but nothing stolen. "Is that why you're here? You think Florence left it with me?"

"She liked you."

"Yes, well, I never acted like an entitled, petulant toddler," Hyde snapped. They were annoyed at Lonnie ruining one of their favourite days of the year. "She didn't. All I've found in my family book relates entirely to vampires. And I'm sure even you are aware Florence wasn't one of us."

"Give it to me, you absolute—" Lonnie's shout took them by surprise. He found himself interrupted by a flying cat. "Blasted furry twit. Get this thing off me."

Hyde was content to watch Mortar and Pestle chase Lonnie out of the shop. The cats sauntered back to them, looking supremely pleased with themselves. "I think you two deserve extra-special treats. Rosa baked up some bat-shaped catnip treats for you."

The biscuits went down well with the cats. They wandered over to lounge in their favourite chairs, rolling around blissfully. Hyde didn't feel as relaxed as they did.

"Everything all right in here?" Vitya stepped into the shop a few minutes later as Hyde was closing up for the evening. "We ran into a cat-scratched Lonnie. The twins are speaking to him. He's confessed to breaking into the taco bus and several cottages in the village. What did you do to him?"

"Me? Nothing. He came in screaming at me. Mortar and Pestle took great offence." Hyde nodded towards the lounging cats. "Will you charge him?"

"Probably. Detective Inspector Filippov will want to question him further. Just wanted to make sure you're okay." Vitya avoided the cats. Some of the shifters in the village had mildly adverse reactions to Mortar and Pestle. Florence had always claimed it was because they had intense energy. "Festival's just getting started. They'll be lighting the bonfire soon."

"I can't wait." Hyde waved him out, then jogged upstairs to grab a thicker cardigan to go underneath their blazer. Mortar and Pestle had remained down-stairs. "I'll leave the door to the flat open if you want to go up."

They ignored her.

Hyde chuckled before heading out of the shop. The scent of orange, cinnamon, and sage filled the air. A few cauldrons bubbled here and there with the herbal mixture intended to cleanse the village for the coming winter.

Standing still for a moment, Hyde breathed in deeply the familiar scent of late October. It was a warm balm against the impending bitter cold. The heaviness that had settled on South Myrddin through the past few weeks had finally vanished.

"Give me a hand? I've served my last taco, so I'm ready to close up for the evening." Teresa drew Hyde out of their thoughts. She waved them over, smiling when they leaned in for a kiss. It was sometimes hard to believe their new normal together. Difficult to comprehend but wonderful. "Let me change my clothes, and then we can head down to the park for the bonfire. I promised I'd sing."

Between the two of them, they managed to clean up the kitchen and shut down the bus. Teresa darted upstairs to change. She came back down in tight jeans, a Wolfsbane concert T-shirt, and her leather jacket for warmth.

Hyde had to clear their throat a few times when Teresa dragged her fingers through her long brown hair, pulling it back into an easy ponytail. "You're beautiful."

"I adore you." Teresa fluffed up Hyde's ginger curls before reaching over to grab an autumn-themed beanie. She gently pulled it down over their head. "I knitted this for you."

Hyde adjusted it a little so some of their curls peeked out of the front. "I love it and you."

They stood awkwardly, staring at each other. Hyde darted in for another kiss, then headed for the door. A chuckling Teresa followed them.

"Hello, you two." Shikoba beckoned them over to her stall on the corner. "Have some spiced apple tea. Ada brought some cider from the orchard, and I've made it into my own concoction."

Hyde wrapped both hands around the cup, soaking in the warmth from the tea. "Smells brilliant."

Moving down the lane towards the park, they stopped at a few other stalls. Rosa handed them a little bag of biscuits. It tided them over until they got to Rees.

"Evening, little duck. I've some extra crispy chips with your name on them." He was, as always, unmoved by their glare. "I can hear your stomach growling."

"You can't." Hyde inspected the bag he handed to them. "My name isn't on this."

Rees growled under his breath and then grabbed the packet. He pulled a pen out of his pocket and scribbled their name before handing it back to them. "Off with you both. Enjoy the bonfire."

Snickering to themselves, they noshed on a packet of chips from the Malt Moon booth on the way down to the bonfire. They'd finished them by the time they got to the park. Hyde tossed the crumpled bag into the recycling bin while Teresa wandered over to join the other musically inclined villagers.

"Going to be a good fire." Emrys sidled up beside them. He pulled a bag of chocolate buttons out of his pocket and offered one to them. "Ah, the thinning of the veil. Past meets present with a nod to the future. May the gods and goddesses keep us safe as we remember those we've lost."

"Florence would've loved this."

"She would, but we'll enjoy it doubly for her." Emrys offered them another chocolate. "I walked the village boundaries with a cleansing flame."

"I feel safer already." Hyde tossed the candy into their mouth. "Are you going to join the singing?"

"Maybe later." Emrys left the bag of candy in Hyde's hand. "I'm happy to see you flourishing, foundling. It's why the village is here—for the lost to find their way."

In his usually enigmatic manner, Emrys disappeared into the crowds, leaving them to ponder his words. Hyde popped a chocolate button into their mouth and decided not to delve too deeply into it. Nothing good could come from deciphering a druid's thoughts.

The strains of a violin pierced the air. The crowd quietened down enough for the haunting beauty of Teresa's voice to be heard. Shivers went down Hyde's spine at the first bars of "Oran na Cloiche."

Midway through the concert around the bonfire, Teresa shifted into painfully familiar folk songs. Ones that had been Florence's absolute favourites. Hyde ignored the tears dripping down their face, smiling through the emotions at the beautiful magic woven through the brisk breeze and crackling fire.

By the end of the night, the embers were still glowing, but everyone had traipsed back home. Hyde stood with Teresa, enjoying the cloudless sky and the lingering warmth.

"Come on. We've said our goodbyes. I'm starving." Teresa slipped her hand into Hyde's. They strolled along the banks of the loch until they found an out-of-the-way spot where they weren't likely to be disturbed. "I've got plenty of blankets. Fynn lent us his portable heater as well."

They retrieved the picnic basket and other things they'd hidden underneath a tree. Hyde spread out one of the blankets on the grass. It was a perfect way to end their Samhain—a romantic meal under the moonlight.

Teresa took a seat beside them on the blanket. She shifted forward, sliding her hand up Hyde's back and drawing them into a kiss. "Have I mentioned that I adore you?"

Before Hyde could respond, a loud splash followed by a shriek of laughter disrupted their peace. They sat up, trying to find the source of the sound. It took a second to spot the two figures floundering around in the water.

"Are you drowning on purpose or in the hopes of being rescued by your one true love?" Teresa snickered.

Hyde frowned. They hadn't immediately recognised the two figures. "Flossie? Winifred? What are you doing? Actually, you know what, I'm not certain I want to know." Their eyes widened. "Oh my gods, you're naked. Why are you starkers? Why? What possible reason could you have to be without clothes when it's freezing outside?"

"I can confirm that it is indeed colder than a witch's—" Flossie squeaked when Winifred swatted her on the arm. "Am I wrong?"

"Mind your language. We shouldn't corrupt the ears of the young ones."

"Why not? We've already ruined their eyes."

Flossie gestured in their direction, chortling when Hyde covered their face. "It's a tradition. We usually go for an icy swim on Yule. This year, we wanted to honour our fallen sister, so we're jumping in a little early."

"And traumatising anyone who might be having a romantic midnight snack," Hyde grumbled.

Teresa leaned into Hyde with a helpless laugh. "Think we'll be like them when we grow up?"

"I'm not sure I'll ever be quite so fearless and fabulous." Hyde continued to avert their eyes from the splashing witches. "Nothing stopping us from being a little like them."

"Hyde." Teresa sighed in resignation.

"For Florence? We can keep our clothes on." Hyde got to their feet. They grinned at Teresa, who muttered to herself before joining them. "Blessed Samhain, Resa."

"A blessed and partly naked Samhain to you." Teresa caught their hand and ran towards the water. "May the coming months be magical and full of love."

BE ON THE LOOK OUT FOR BOOK TWO, A FATAL Autumnal Stew.

ACKNOWLEDGMENTS

A massive thank-you to my brilliant betas and the crew in my Cozies by the Fire group who helped brainstorm some of the names in the book. To Becky, Kristin, and all the fantastic people at Tangled Tree and Hot Tree Publishing. And also to my beloved hubby who keeps me from losing my mind while I'm stressing over word counts.

And lastly, thank you, readers, for following me on my writing journey. I hope you enjoyed *A Curse for Samhain* and are looking forward to book two.

ABOUT THE AUTHOR

Dahlia Donovan wrote her first romance series after a crazy dream about shifters and damsels in distress. She prefers irreverent humour and unconventional characters. An autistic and occasional hermit, her life wouldn't be complete without her husband and her massive collection of books and video games.

Don't miss out on new releases, exclusive giveaways, and much more!

Join Dahlia's newsletter:

http://eepurl.com/Q0n0X

Join her reader group:

www.facebook.com/groups/1108750876162947

She'd love to hear from you directly, too. Please feel free to email her at dahlia@dahliadonovan.com or check out her website https://dahliadonovan.com/ for updates.

facebook.com/dahliadonovan

x.com/DahliaDonovan

instagram.com/dahliadonovanauthor

pinterest.com/dahliadonovan

ABOUT THE PUBLISHER

Hot Tree Publishing loves love. Publishing adult romantic fiction, HTPubs are all about diverse reads featuring heroes and heroines to swoon over. Since opening in 2015, HTPubs have published more than 300 titles across the wide and diverse range of romantic genres. If you're chasing a happily ever after in your favourite subgenre, HTPubs have you covered.

Interested in discovering more amazing reads brought to you by Hot Tree Publishing? Head over to the website for information:

WWW.HOTTREEPUBLISHING.COM

facebook.com/hottreepublishing

x.com/hottreepubs

instagram.com/hottreepublishing